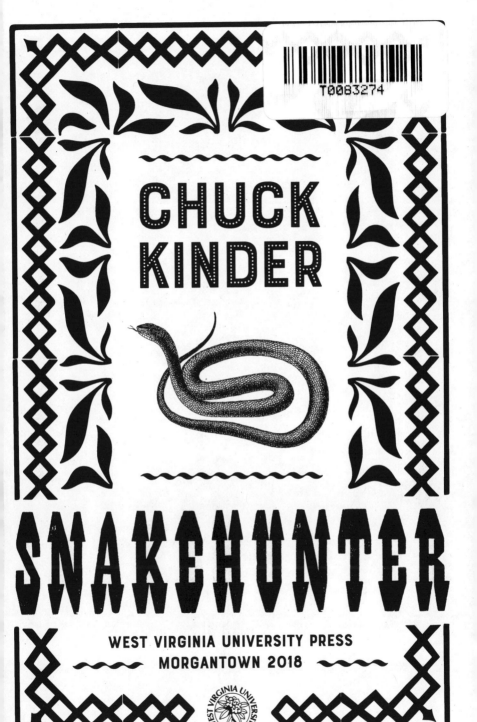

CHUCK KINDER

SNAKEHUNTER

WEST VIRGINIA UNIVERSITY PRESS
MORGANTOWN 2018

First edition published 1973
by Knopf
Second edition published 1991
by Gnomon Press
Third edition published 2018
by West Virginia University Press

Printed in the United States of America

ISBN:
Paper 978-1-946684-53-0
Ebook 978-1-946684-54-7

Library of Congress Cataloging-in-Publication Data
Names: Kinder, Chuck, author.
Title: Snakehunter / Chuck Kinder.
Description: Third edition. | Morgantown : West Virginia University Press, 2018.
Identifiers: LCCN 2018019666| ISBN 9781946684530
        (paper) | ISBN 9781946684547 (ebook)
Subjects: LCSH: West Virginia--Fiction. | BISAC: FICTION / General.
Classification: LCC PS3561.I426 S64 2018 | DDC 813/.54--dc20
LC record available at https://lccn.loc.gov/2018019666

Cover design by Than Saffel / WVU Press

*This hillbilly book is for my mountain beauties—
Diane, Daisy, Pearl, Eileen, Nancy Beth,
Morgan Ann, Amy Beth, and little Lulu*

Snakehunter

Prologue

Dear old Pop.

My dear old Pop's name was Speer Whitfield. I am his namesake. Because they were second cousins my dear old Ma's maiden name was also Whitfield, Mary Jane Whitfield. When I was a squirt this fact confused me somewhat. Before he got his in the end by a single bullet in a French forest, my Pop had been a coal miner and then later after many years of night school a high school English teacher. I have several pictures of him, so in a sense I know what he looked like: tall and dark, and in an angular way somewhat handsome I guess. It is his eyes, though, in these pictures which most come to life for me when I study his thin face, the way they look darkly out at me, the way they seem to be trying to fasten themselves to my own eyes. When I was a squirt I used to pretend to others and even to myself that I could actually recall him. I used to make up lots of happy memories about him. For a time I pretended like he was not really dead at all, only invisible, and that he was actually with me always. Whenever I played army I pretended that dear old Pop was my captain and that whatever I did, I did on top secret orders straight from him. He led my attacks. He covered my retreats. He carried me off the battlefield whenever I was wounded. I outgrew these stupid games of course. I haven't pretended that dear old Pop is my hot shit hero for years, years.

I can remember Ma showing my sister Cynthia and me several photographs of a field which was filled with rows upon rows of crosses. There were no trees at all in that field, not even in the distance, only crosses and crosses which in some of the pictures, because of the shots' angles, created strange optical effects, giving illusions of undulating serpentine lines. One particular cross, always in the various pictures' foregrounds, had been faintly marked with ink. This

Ma told us was our dear old Pop's grave. The field of crosses is in France. France is across an ocean. I have been told that my dear old Pop was brave and that he died a hero's death. Maybe this is true. I don't see how it matters, though, one way or the other. Dead is dead. Besides, heroes have always given me a pain in the ass. Anyway, that's all she wrote for dear old Pop.

Dear old Ma.

Ma was going to break into showbiz and become a star and get rich and famous. She was a cinch, folks said, because she was a deadringer for Lauren Bacall.

I remember a long bridge, buildings with windows liquid gold in a late afternoon sun's light, pigeons eating popcorn in the grass. They could turn their heads all the way around. Ma said to stay away from them because they were dirty and carried lice. Once some negro boys chased Cynthia and me in the park. Ma said not to ever go back there unless she was with us. His house was big and looked like a castle or something. His name was J. P. Morgan but he was dead. There was a mummy there and lots of men in iron suits. The sidewalks were hot and had steaming dog shit all over them. I saw some lions and tigers. They walked back and forth. Behind the glass were lots of snakes which gave me the shivers. A policeman was on a horse. Once a man was lying by the curb and a fat woman was kicking him. She kicked him again and again and the people around them laughed. Where we lived was hot. Our little fan turned from side to side but it was still hot. Where we lived was up a lot of stairs. Ma brought us home a goldfish in a little cardboard carton but it floated up on its side and was dead. Then she brought us home a little turtle. Its shell was painted blue. It got away.

A man came to stay with us who had black hair. He was a boarder, Ma told us, who would help us pay our rent. After a time he went away. Ma brought us home another goldfish but once when Cynthia was cleaning its water in the bathroom sink the stopper came out and the fish went down the drain. It wasn't dead though, Cynthia said. She said that the fish would swim through the sewers until it finally reached the river where it would be all right again.

A man came who had red hair and freckles all over his skin. His hands were big and I watched his strong fingers tighten around beer cans, crushing them easily. I pictured his hands squeezing my head in. Once while he was on the commode, Cynthia and I opened the bathroom door and stood there watching him. The commode was across the room from the door and he couldn't reach it without getting up. Cynthia laughed and pointed at him and told him he looked like a fat squatty toad. He shouted at us. Then Ma came and closed the door. She tried to act mad but she was grinning. Ma brought us home another little turtle with a blue shell. At last the red-headed man went away and we were all glad.

When it got cold Ma banged on the radiator with her shoe. We wore blankets over our shoulders and stayed a lot of the time in the same bed together. Sometimes in the evenings we would listen to the radio and Ma would play-act along with our favorite programs, making crazy voices and hopping all over the bed. I can clearly picture her face as she laughs and talks: a photograph that becomes fluid, becomes film for me. Her gray eyes far apart, hair long and dark, the wide smiling mouth, full lips that I put in motion. She has a million facial expressions. When I concentrate on her face while she speaks I can make it constantly change, alter to share the showbiz of what she says. Often she makes funny faces for us. We laugh. She can touch her nose with her tongue. We laugh. Ma is a real card. Sometimes she tells us ghost stories. Sometimes she tells us these stories late at night while we all sit with the covers pulled over our heads like a tent. Ma holds a flashlight in her lap with its beam directed up over her face making strange shadows. She makes sounds like old doors creaking open and shut or like dead people moaning from moldy graves.

"Tell us about vampires again," Cynthia says.

"Ah yes," Ma says, doing her spooky Bela Lugosi imitation, which of all the dozens of imitations she can do is my favorite. "When the moon is full they rise from their coffins and stalk around the countryside in search of blood. Human blood. Warm wonderful blood that they suck from the necks of their victims. But in the end even vampires get what's coming to them. With a stake pounded in the heart or with a silver bullet in the brain ha ha hee hee hee ha ha hee hee hee hee ha ha!"

If Cynthia and I get too scared, Ma starts tickling us and we all laugh. In the mornings we find ice frozen on the windows.

The red-headed man came back. He slapped Cynthia but she didn't cry. I cried but she didn't and he hadn't even slapped me. Then he hit Ma. She fell down. Cynthia threw a can at him. His head was bleeding. He kicked over our turtle's box then he stomped on our turtle. He went away. Ma vomited over and over. I cried and Ma cried but Cynthia didn't. Cynthia scraped up the turtle from the linoleum with a knife. She said that she was going to make some turtle soup with it but I knew she wasn't really. I knew that she was about to cry too.

We could hear rats running in the walls at night. Sometimes they would come out from behind the stove in the kitchen. Cynthia threw things at them. Once she hit one with a broom and it went around and around in circles. It was long and black and its fur looked shiny. Then she hit it again. Its back legs wouldn't work. She hit it again. I ran away. She said for me to come look at it again but I wouldn't.

Finally it got warm again and Cynthia and I could play outdoors on the sidewalk. A lot of the people around where we lived talked funny. A lot of the people would watch Cynthia and me as we walked along the street. They would stare at Cynthia's face which had cancer. I was always worried that the red-headed man would come back and hit us some more but he never did.

Memory.
Once while taking a long, beer-foamy leak in a bar's head, I read scribbled on one of its walls some graffiti which said that "reality is the shifting face of need." I know from my own experience that the past is the only truly controllable reality. Also, I know from my own experience that there are responsibilities which I owe to myself that begin with my memory.

One

Century.

We had no choice about it, Ma said. She didn't want to any more than we did, but we were going to have to do it. But at least we would have enough money to go to the movies a lot like we used to. We had not been able to go to many movies for a long time but now we could. That was something anyway, wasn't it? "If we can't break into the goddamn movies at least we can go to them again, my little chickadees," Ma said in her funny W. C. Fields voice. But we were still sad.

So we were going to live again with my Great-Aunt Erica in her big house on Kanawha Street in Century, West Virginia. Aunt Erica said that we could stay just as long as we wanted because she was well aware that Ma had to have ample time to "find herself" and to "get her feet on the ground again." We wouldn't stay there too long and Aunt Erica wouldn't boss us around, Ma promised Cynthia and me. But neither of these things turned out to be true, of course. We ended up living there a long time, even after Ma remarried. We ended up living there so long that it seemed like we had never lived anyplace else in the whole world.

Grandpaw lived there too, but he spent most of his time in his old trailer out behind the house on the concrete foundation of a large chicken coop he had once built but which had long ago burned down. He needed his privacy away from all the gabby females, he said, and meant it, and so when he wasn't working in his vegetable garden, he sat in an old, large, stuffed green chair pulled to the door of his trailer just chewing and spitting tobacco and sipping moonshine from a mason jar. Catherine, a wondrous, crazy cousin who drank to excess, lived there also. She was the high school librarian and she had her own private apartment in two of the large downstairs rooms of the house. She had lived with Aunt

Erica for many years, her parents having died in their Buick's burning wreckage when she was just eleven; her father, a federal judge no less, had been Aunt Erica's and Grandpaw's youngest brother. Uncle Charlie, Ma's older brother, lived with his family, with Hilda and their son Henry and Hilda's various visiting relatives, in another house Aunt Erica owned, directly across the street from us. It was a real shitpot clan sort of situation.

Aunt Erica's house was large and old, its style a sort of self-conscious Victorian (a half-hearted turret, strange half-moon windows of stained glass above various massive doors, etc.). It was a frame house with porches along one side and along the front, and with a glassed-in back porch. There were broad yards on all sides and old trees around, some so near the house their branches squeaked ghostily against the upstairs windows' glass and brushed the white boards in the wind with sounds like rats running in the walls at night. It was the first house built not only on Kanawha Street but in the whole west end of Century: built jointly by Aunt Erica and her older brother, Dr. Alfonso Whitfield, who had been dead ever since he dispatched his brains with a bullet on December 7, 1941, and whose name Aunt Erica managed to mention at least a half-dozen times in the course of a single day.

I liked Catherine and Uncle Charlie and Grandpaw, forming my alliances with them right off the bat. Aunt Hilda and Henry were my main enemies. About Aunt Erica, I was never sure. I liked her and hated her by turns, depending on whether her dictates went for or against my needs. Aunt Erica was just Aunt Erica and learning to get along with her was like learning a shuffling dance step. The only good thing about this was that you weren't dancing around alone. Not by a long shot. There were a lot of people who knew how to step lightly to Aunt Erica's tune. And not just the family either. She had been president of the Methodist Women's

Bible Class for over thirty years. She was president of the town's Woman's Club and of the local chapters of both the D.A.R. and the Eastern Star. I could go on, but you get the picture. She virtually ruled the clucking old lady power structure of the small town's society. She wasn't, however, a hard woman who just sat around coldly calculating how to have her way in things. And she didn't really manipulate people. It was just a question of energy, I think. And also a question of getting things done in a practical way. She was a practical woman all right. In fact, it was her biggest pride and about her only boast. She claimed that she was the most practical woman who had ever lived. Or close to it anyway.

"You have to be practical to get through life," she used to say. "If you're not practical you can't make do with a thing. And I always say there is a blessing of God about practical ways of doing things."

I can think of only one way in which Aunt Erica was not steadfastly practical. And that had to do with her quite expensive collection of seventeen tombstones. But then we all have some sort of hobby, I guess. Even Aunt Erica.

Turtle Bottom.

For all the years when it was just a river bank settlement the town had been known as Turtle Bottom. Later, it had become the coal mining boom town of Hundred Mines. When the mines finally began playing out or mechanizing in the late 1930s, the town had been renamed again as Century.

A strange rock turtle is on exhibition at the Smithsonian Institute in Washington, D.C.: a rather large one, which was apparently carved from solid stone by some prehistoric race of Indians. It was uncovered on a stretch of bottom-land beside the Kanawha River in southern West Virginia during a large flood in the early 1800s. According to reports of the time, a burial ground was revealed. Besides whole skeletons, piles upon piles of bones and skulls were found, and even a clay pot which held over two hundred human teeth. It appeared as though the dead had been deliberately placed so that their heads were pointed toward the stone turtle. For many years after the flood this stretch of land was called Turtle Bottom by the local folks.

Hundred Mines.

In order to obtain the cheapest labor possible, the coal companies recruited men in foreign lands with promises of great opportunity. Once, a train of cattle cars had carried over two hundred Italians into the valley, few of whom could read, write, or even speak any English at all.

At one time the town had seven times the number of saloons as churches and more unnatural deaths than natural. According to a saying of the time, there was no Sunday west of Clifton Forge, Virginia; and there was no God west of Hinton, West Virginia.

Vigilante law was not unknown, and there were several recorded lynchings. Once, a black dude was mutilated for having made approaches to a white woman. After a long, late-night chase through the streets and alleys of the negro section of town, the young black had been caught, stripped naked, then tied to a lamp post. There, in the bright circle of light, a member of the mob had used a knife on the man's organs, literally carving them away. Catherine told me about this, and she told me that the man with the knife was an infamous badman of that day, a certain Mr. Slick, who was called this both because of his absolute baldness and because of his slick use of a blade. Would you believe that this Mr. Slick, Catherine said, was better known to me as Grandpaw.

Century.

To enter the town of Century from either the east or the west end (the south and north being bordered respectively by the river and the mountains), you pass through streets lined with small single-story frame houses, built exactly the same. Once they were coal company houses. Now only negro families live in them and many are boarded up. Their coal-blackened dirt yards grow thickly with patches of wild grass and weeds, and are littered with rubbish: rusted-out bodies of old cars, ancient appliances, mattress springs, old tires. Most of the houses' walls are weather-streaked, paint long peeled away, the wide, vertically lapped boards often as slick as bones, the occasional tar paper patches like black sores.

A few of the houses, however, have been freshly soaked with whitewash. Although coal dust film settles quickly over them, these houses stand starkly bright among the others. Usually the plank fences or the rowed stones which mark these houses' raked and swept yards are also whitewashed. In several yards there are brightly colored plaster of paris bird-baths. Sometimes there are artificial chickens or ducks set about the yards as though they are headed some place in particular.

January 1949.

Ma carries me down the narrow metal steps into the cold air. The train is dripping underneath and steaming along its sides. We see Uncle Charlie waiting on the platform for us. He is tall and thin and has a dark mustache and wears thick rimless glasses. A couple of soldiers are also on the platform, their winter coats deep brown, long and heavy, and with shining brass buttons. Uncle Charlie wears a tweed overcoat and has no hat. He smiles and waves to us.

"Well look who we have here," he says as he walks toward us. His breath rises like smoke into the air.

"You mean look what the damn cat has drug in," Ma says, as Uncle Charlie hugs and kisses her.

"Mary Jane," he says, "you are a pretty sight for sore eyes. You just keep getting better-looking all the time. Well, it's good to have you home again, girl."

"Yas, dahling," Ma says in her Tallulah Bankhead voice, "how divine to see you. But don't forget, dahling, this is only a visit. It's only a little breather."

Uncle Charlie lifts Cynthia up and kisses her. Then he lifts me up, holds me out from him, looking me over. My nose is running. There are small beads of ice in his mustache and in his heavy black eyebrows. Through his thick glasses his eyes look watery and swollen.

"Hey, this couldn't be little Speer. Not this big fellow."

"That's him all right," Ma says. "Isn't he a big boy?"

"I'll say. I'll bet he takes good care of his Mom, doesn't he?"

"He's his old lady's little mannie all right," Ma says.

Uncle Charlie puts me down. People are watching us, but they turn their eyes away when I look back at them. I look at Ma and Uncle Charlie to see if they see the people watching too, but their faces don't show anything. My face stings from the wind and I press it into the wool folds of Ma's coat.

"I'll fetch up the bags," Uncle Charlie says. "You all wait inside the depot where it's warm."

"Why don't we just wait out here?" Ma says. "We'll just wait here."

"No, now you folks better go on in."

"Really, darling, I think we'll just tarry around here."

"Now we can't have that, ma'am. Youall will freeze your behinds off out here. Now youall just go on in and I'll be there directly."

"Oh well, what the hell," Ma says.

We go through the small crowd of people on the platform toward the double doors of the depot, which are glass-paned and are steamed over. My breath gets sucked away when we step from the cold air into the hot, stuffed room. Even through my clogged nose comes the heavy mingled smells of breath and bodies and clothes. Smoke spreads through the single room of the waiting area and collects in bluish clouds toward the high ceiling. As soon as we came into the room people began to look at us again and I look up to see if Ma sees them this time, but just as usual she doesn't. She directs Cynthia and me close along the cream-colored plastered wall toward a low window where we stop to stand and wait. The glass panes of the window are steamed also, and I cannot see out onto the platform. For a long time I stand facing the window, drawing funny faces on the misted glass, which feels cool and slick. Finally I turn around again to the room.

They are still watching.

Where is Uncle Charlie? I wonder. It seems like a long time. There are several rows of benches running parallel to our wall, each row fixed like two long church pews put back to back. Their wood is dull, looking smudged and oily and as though it would feel sticky. Several kids are running through the aisles between the benches laughing and tagging at one another. When they see us they stop and look. Then a red-headed boy with bright freckles laughs. They all laugh and turn and run off. I look at Ma's face but it is the same.

The women watch. There are four of them sitting along the bench nearest to where we stand. They have full, red meaty faces and wear old cloth coats which are spread open, showing print dresses. They watch us. I wonder where Uncle Charlie is. I don't look at the fat slobs. At one end of the room on the wall above the ticket office is a large round clock whose long hand jerks noticeably from black minute mark to mark. When I look closely at the glass of its face I can see reflected wavering figures from the room, and, vaguely, even the faces of those people nearest to it. They look like weird underwater fish faces pressed close to the glass sides of a bowl.

"Poor thing."

I didn't even see the man walk up. He stands almost directly in front of Ma. But she doesn't seem to have seen or heard him. Her eyes are still settled straight ahead as though fixed upon something important on the far wall, or even beyond the wall, fixed so far away that her eyes have gone empty. Then she gives a little jerk, suddenly surprised to find someone so close to us.

"How did it happen?" the man asks, patting Cynthia on the head.

Cynthia slaps at his hand.

"Go away," Ma says.

I can feel cold air rising off his clothing and a strange sour smell comes from him too. The front of his old coat is held together with safety pins. He needs a shave and his eyes are very wet. I can feel the people in the room watching us.

"Go away. Please," Ma says.

"Poor, poor little thing."

"You're drunk. Now get the hell away from us."

"Poor little girly," the man says, again patting Cynthia's head.

"Get your smelly hand away," Cynthia says and takes a kick at him.

Uncle Charlie walks quickly up to us.

"What's the problem here?"

"Get this goddamn drunken pig away from us before I scratch his goddamn eyes out," Ma says in a low, scratchy voice.

"Why, I didn't mean no harm, Charlie," the man says to Uncle Charlie in a high quivery voice. "Honest, Charlie."

"Get this goddamn pig out of here!"

"All right now. Everyone just settle down," Uncle Charlie says in a very quiet, calm voice.

"Honest to God, Charlie," the man says. "I didn't mean no harm."

"All right, Bill. All right. It's all right. It's just a misunderstanding. Now you just go on along and everything will be fine. Go on now."

"What the hell do you mean by 'all right'?" Ma says to Uncle Charlie after the man turns and walks slowly away. "That goddamn pig. I could strangle the bastard."

"Well, just forget it now. That was only old Boomer Bill. He's harmless. It's all over now, honey. Let's head on home."

"He was a goddamn pig, Charlie. You sure haven't changed much have you?"

Uncle Charlie's eyelids look droopy like he is sleepy or something and he has a strange little smile on his lips.

"Well, old Boomer Bill didn't mean to cause you any difficulty. He's not fully responsible for what he does. Years ago, before his health broke in the mines at Boomer, he was a good hard-working man. He's had a lot of bad luck."

"Well, if he ever gets close to me again, he'll find out what bad luck is all about."

January 1949, contd.

My nose was running beyond the point where I could with a good deep breath suck the mucus back up into my nostrils and throat and swallow it. I had to breathe in the freezing air through my mouth and my teeth ached with chill. Uncle Charlie carried the two suitcases and walked ahead and we followed down the narrow footpath that had been beaten through the snow on the sidewalk. His heavy galoshes crushed easily through the crust of the old snow, whose whiteness had grayed with coal dust. The trees along the street seemed very black in the washed-out, white air. Their dark limbs were hung with frozen, powdery snow which with each gust of wind sprayed down upon our heads and shoulders in a fine cloud. We turned in at the front gate. Uncle Charlie had seeded the snow on the long walk with salt and I could feel its tiny crystals crunch as delicately as glass under my steps all the way up to the porch.

"Well, home sweet home and all that bullshit," Ma said.

"The prodigal returns," Uncle Charlie said, turning his head and smiling.

"So where's the goddamn slaughtered calf I'd like to know? Where's the festivities? Where's the booze?"

"You've picked up a New York Jew accent. Talk through your beak."

"So I ask you, what's wrong with that for chrissake?"

Aunt Erica came out onto the porch carrying a broom. She was a lot smaller than I remembered her. She was a flurry of quick movements. She looked almost spastic as she hurried to the top of the steps, elbows jerking around like stunted wings, her head bobbing about like a chicken pecking the air after strange floating seeds.

"I swand! I just swand! I just swand to gracious! Just look who we got coming up the walk! Look who we got here! All my sweetie dumplings!"

"Right. Just look," Ma said. "The strays return repentant to the flock."

"Oh it's so good to have you all home. Oh welcome back again. I've missed you I've missed you. Oh Mary Jane my sweetie pie come here come here. Let me hug the daylights out of you. Oh the babies the babies. Let me just gobble gobble them right up this minute."

"Help yourself," Ma said, laughing. "Youall remember your Auntie Erica, don't you kids?"

"Are you kidding?" Cynthia whispered to me just before Aunt Erica put an arm around each of us and pulled us to her.

"Well, let's all get right inside before we freeze to ice," Aunt Erica said, letting Cynthia and me loose. "And don't none of you all go tracking in on my rugs. Charlie, you get those wet boots off. Here, sweep off with this broom. Land's sake, just look at this little boy's nose. Now one of you could have taken time to wipe this little child's nose. It's going right in his little mouth."

"He's partial to snot," Ma said.

I sat back in the darkness of the corner by the refrigerator and played that I was inside a secret cave from where I could look out at the kitchen as though I was not really a part of it. Ma and Catherine and Uncle Charlie and Aunt Hilda and Grandpaw were all sitting or standing around talking while Aunt Erica flurried about the room getting supper together. As usual she had refused all offers of help, preferring to do everything herself. Catherine had given me a shoebox full of seashells to play with and so I just sat there on the floor scooting them around like they were small ships following the colored swirling patterns of the linoleum sea. Naturally I was picking up on everything said by the grownups. I was one of those nosy brat kids who was always sneaking around spying on people. That was sort of my hobby, I guess.

Uncle Charlie stood over beside the pot-bellied coal stove, his back toward the hot iron sides. There was a slight steamed smell of clothes, of flannel and corduroy. From his shirt pocket, Uncle Charlie took out a long Havana cigar. He slipped off the ringlike gold seal, skinned away the crinkling clear cellophane, wet the outer brown leaves with his tongue until they darkened moistly, put it securely between his teeth and lit it, drawing deeply, the smoke hovering about his face before finally rising as he waved his hand through it.

"Don't start that stuff already," he said to Aunt Hilda.

"I'm talking to Mary Jane," Aunt Hilda said.

"For pete's sake, she just got here," Uncle Charlie said.

"I'm not addressing you, mister," Hilda said. She was sitting in the heavy oak rocker near the stove. Her hair looked like glowing orange filaments in the kitchen's bright overhead light; her makeup creased darkly along her heavy face's wrinkles. She looked like a real creep. She was rocking slowly back and forth, stringing green beans which she took one by one from a paper sack on her lap, snapping off their crisp, pale ends, dropping the beans then into a metal straining bowl which rested balanced on her knees. Every so often Aunt Erica would stop as she passed Hilda and take a few beans from the bowl and look them over carefully to see if they met her standards. She would just ignore Hilda's glare.

"We don't have to start choosing up sides tonight," Uncle Charlie said, his voice so quiet as usual that you could hardly hear it.

"Let me stay out of it," Ma said. She was sitting at the kitchen table with Catherine.

"Charlie, I am addressing Mary Jane I told you," Hilda said. "And I asked her don't it just take the cake. Can you believe a body getting offered one thousand dollars for one stupid tree and not jumping at the chance? That's good old Charlie for you. Don't it just beat the band? One thousand dollar bills in cold cash and he wouldn't let them cut it down."

"Let me stay out of it," Ma said. "It's none of my business."

"That tree is a black walnut," Uncle Charlie said. "Over three feet in diameter. You just don't find trees like that anymore."

"Three feet in diameter! Three feet in diameter!" Aunt Hilda snorted. "Well, that news just makes my heart go pitty-pat!"

"I'd think you'd have some empathy for anything that size," Uncle Charlie said. Ma and Catherine laughed.

"You're just begging for more trouble than you can handle, mister!" Hilda said. "You just keep it up!"

"Charlie may have a historical precedent," Catherine said.

"Nobody asked for your two-cents' worth as I recall," Hilda said.

"Indeed," Catherine said, taking a drink of something

from a big brown mug, her long, pale face drawing to a kiss-like pinch at her lips each time she sipped.

"Why don't everone just quiet down," Grandpaw said from over where he was sitting alone by one of the broad side windows. He spit in the blue and red Maxwell House coffee can he often used as a spittoon. With the back of one of his huge hands he wiped several thin brown strings of juice from the white stubble on his chin. "I can't hardly hear my radio show," he said, and hunched over nearer the cathedral-shaped front of the old Philco.

"What precedent were you referring to, learned cousin?" Charlie asked in almost a whisper. Everyone except Hilda and Aunt Erica and Grandpaw was smiling. Hilda had stopped rocking and was just sitting there glaring at Catherine who didn't even seem to notice. Aunt Erica, just busying around the kitchen humming softly to herself, didn't appear to be listening at all.

"Well," Catherine said, speaking in that weird, shrill, sing-song voice of hers and clearing her throat often, "long ago in ancient Germany if one so much as peeled the bark of a living tree the authorities would cut one's navel out and nail it promptly to the damaged tree. Then one found one's self run forcibly around and around it until one's insides were wound about its trunk. In other words, one played ring-around-the-rosy with one's guts."

"Goddamn that's gruesome," Ma said, laughing.

"It dang sure is," Grandpaw said, slapping his leg and laughing also until he got choked on tobacco juice and started to cough.

"Oh, Mary Jane," Aunt Erica said, turning around sharply from the cabinet's wooden workboard where she had started kneading dough. "Oh my gracious, how awful you have learned to talk. Taking the Lord's name in vain. I swand to gracious if you were a little girl I would wash your mouth out with soap this very instant."

"Golly gee," Ma said. "So sorry, Auntie."

"Well," Hilda said, getting up heavily from the rocker. "It seems to me that there's other folks around here with a lot more garbage in their mouths than Mary Jane. Now that's my opinion."

"I'll toast that astute observation," Catherine said, smiling, and then took a long pull from the big mug.

"Down the old perverbial hatch," Uncle Charlie said, taking a drink from a bottle of beer which he had just opened. "I'll swill along with you on that, Kitty old girl."

"I'll tell you what you'll do, Charlie," Aunt Erica said. "You'll put out that smelly cigar. It's stinking up my kitchen to high heavens."

"Well, I'm aheadin' out back," Grandpaw said, getting stiffly up from his chair. "Maybe I can hear my radio show out there. Someone bring me my supper when it's fixed if it ain't too much bother."

"Well you might or might not get your supper out back," Aunt Erica said. "Eating out in that old cold trailer like some sort of nigger! You crazy old bird!"

Trees.

In Allumba, in central Australia, there is a tree to which the sun, in the shape of a woman, is said to have traveled from the east. The natives believe that if the tree was ever destroyed they would all be burned up in horrible flames.

The Dieri tribe of South Australia regards as very sacred certain trees which are supposed to be their fathers transformed from death. Therefore, they speak with great reverence to those trees and take care not to cut them down or burn them.

The Dyaks believe that when a man dies by accident, as by drowning, it is a sign that the gods mean to exclude him from the realms of heaven. Accordingly, his body is not buried, but is carried into the deep forest and there left. The souls of such unfortunates pass into trees or animals or fish, and they are much dreaded by the Dyaks, who abstain from using certain kinds of wood, or eating certain sorts of fish and animals, because they are supposed to contain the souls of the dead.

The Lkuñgen Indians of British Columbia believe that trees are transformed men, and that the creaking of the branches in the wind is their voices.

Because Uncle Charlie was a private consulting forester, one of only eleven in the whole state, he was very concerned with forest conservation and with what he called intelligent timber-cutting. This was many years before such a concern was fashionable and it seemed like he was always into some running conflict with someone or other. He was also always running for this or that public office and always getting soundly trounced. Catherine was usually his campaign manager, and what county power groups Uncle Charlie didn't rub the wrong way, she did. If it had not been for Aunt Erica's long-entrenched power those two would have probably been run out of town on a rail on several occasions.

When my Great-Uncle Albert, the oldest of Aunt Erica's surviving brothers, sold the timber rights of his part of the family land one spring, in order to finance his campaign for the state senate, Uncle Charlie had refused to sell his share and had persuaded Aunt Erica and Grandpaw not to sell theirs. Then, after the timber crews had finished and gone the next fall, Uncle Charlie and Grandpaw took me with them to see what had been done. We spent two hours walking the ridges and hills of the depleted woods. Uncle Charlie told us that the bastard logging contractors had high-graded the timber, which meant that they had come in and cut away all but the worst trees, leaving only the poor and deformed timber. And now this bad timber would take all the available space and food and moisture and so some day there would be nothing left but squirrel dens. And the loggers had built poor timber roads, Uncle Charlie said. The sort of roads that would erode the topsoil and wash into the bottoms with the spring thaws and rains. The goddamn robber-baron bastards, Uncle Charlie said, and said that Uncle Albert should be horsewhipped for getting in on such a deal. And I can remember Uncle Charlie's angry eyes. Even from behind his thick glasses they looked black and brittle-hard like coal nuggets, and were unblinking, and had his bushy brows shadowing heavily over them.

Before they cut down a great tree, the Indians of Santiago Tepehuacan hold a festival in order to please it. So, too, when the Dyaks fell the jungle on the hills, they often leave a few trees standing on the hilltops as a refuge for the dispossessed tree-spirits.

The Sundanese of the Eastern Archipelago drive golden or silver nails into the trunk of a sacred tree for the sake of expelling the tree-spirit before they hew down his abode. They seem to think that, though the nails will hurt him, his vanity will be soothed by the thought that they are gold or silver.

I remember one fall when fires burned in the hills for two solid weeks before rains at last put them out. In the nights the bright yellow streaks of the fires had weaved like flaming snakes along the dark ridges and swells of the mountains south of the river. The smoke had made the bottoms' nights even darker than usual and the sky looked smudged except for the glow in the south and there had been no stars. In the early evenings the family had gathered on Aunt Erica's front porch to watch the fires burning in the hills directly across the river. I recall how distant and yet how clear those fires seemed. I recall how quiet we all were sitting there on the porch.

Uncle Charlie had gone along with the other volunteers of the valley into the high woods to fight the blazes during this time. On the third night of the fires, Grandpaw had taken me with him to the mouth of Morris Hollow where the supply trucks were parked. He had also taken along a gallon of Ike Williams' moonshine, reputedly the best of the bottoms. Very late that night, Uncle Charlie had come down out of the hills, dark and smoke-grimed and ash-smeared, and had sat down heavily, bone-tired, on the running board of one of the trucks. He had sat quietly looking straight ahead into the darkness as though from some place far away, as though he was not really sitting on the truck's running board in the chilling night air at all, but was strangely far away from himself and was looking back through time to how he had once been. And, suddenly, while watching Uncle Charlie's face and eyes, especially his eyes, I had one of my weird-kid thoughts that maybe dead people's eyes were like that: looked strangely back like Uncle Charlie's eyes looked.

Grandpaw had given me a cup of whiskey to carry to Uncle Charlie but as I watched him I began to feel strangely shy, and even scared, and I walked up to him very timidly. But then, when I finally reached him, I just thrust the cup up in front of his face. Uncle Charlie blinked and looked slowly up to me. For what seemed like a long time he just looked into my face. He looked at me like I was a stranger to him. Then, finally, he smiled, and I dropped the cup of whiskey as I sprang into his arms and against his bearded face. I can remember the brittleness of the salt frost on his flannel shirt and the musk smell of sweat and smoke, and his large hard hand patting against my back.

January 1949, contd.

Aunt Erica sliced her food into small bits, her fork clinking in nervous frequent stabs against the china. With seemingly great concentration she studied the finely minced food before finally singling out those morsels to be eaten. Then,

daintily, she stabbed at each selected bite for several moments before at last spearing it quickly to her mouth. She
chewed with great concentration also, and her dentures
clicked. When not occupied with her food, her eyes darted
constantly around the table, checking out the faces, the
plates, what was eaten and how.

"Mary Jane, you surely haven't broken your neck to teach
these children their table manners," Aunt Erica said.

"Slipped my mind."

"Speer, you use a fork and knife on that chicken," Aunt
Erica told me. "And, Cynthia, that applies to you, too."

"You're not my boss," Cynthia said.

"That's enough, Daughter," Ma said. "Now youall do as
your Aunt Erica says."

"You told us that she wasn't going to boss us around,"
Cynthia said.

"I said that that's enough and I mean it."

"For pete's sake, let them eat with their fingers," Uncle
Charlie said. "They're just kids. Besides everyone eats chicken
with their fingers. Except at this table."

"That's right, except at this table," Aunt Erica said. "It
just looks downright piggy and it spreads grease all over my
good tablecloth. And there's never a time for children to
learn like the present. You know what they say about manners being next to morals."

"I'm not a Biblical scholar," Catherine said, gesturing
with a big chicken leg in her hand. "But I'm sure I read some-
place where some textual authority claims that not only did
Jesus probably chaw his fowl with his fingers but he also
probably licked them clean."

"Oh, Kitty Whitfield," Aunt Erica said, putting down her
fork. "You talk so profane. What an example you set for
these children."

"Well, I shall proceed to remove my corrupting influ-
ence," Catherine said, and got up from the table. "Besides I'm

stuffed as a hog ready for market. I'm proceeding directly
out that front door for a constitutional."

"You're not going out walking in this weather I should
hope," Aunt Erica said. "Folks will think you are strange."

"Dear Auntie, folks know that I'm strange."

"Well, just where are you going may I ask?"

"After all those beastly beans I devoured I'm proceeding
out to break a healthy bag of wind. I fully intend to pollute
the neighborhood from end to end. I will melt the snow from
the trees."

"That kind of talk just downright makes me sick," Hilda
mumbled through a stuffed mouth.

"Home, home on the range," Ma said.

I watched once while Aunt Erica gave it to a chicken. When
she first entered the gate the two dozen or so birds, sensing
danger I guess, scattered in chaotic swarms about the
wired-in dirt yard. Somewhat randomly, she selected a plump
hen and quickly started to close in on it. Although Aunt
Erica was a small woman who at times looked almost frail,
she was quite strong, with forearms as large as some men's.
And she always moved very quickly in what looked like a
flurry of disorganized gestures; but they weren't disorganized
at all, really, and in the heart of that flurry were movements
decisively precise. She had no trouble cornering her selected
hen, and as it made a last desperate scramble to get around
her, she clubbed it silly with the long hoe handle that she had
carried for the purpose. Then, while the bird was stunned,
she grabbed it by its feet and carried it head-down from the
yard. The bird stroked its white wings awkwardly, upside-
down, as though trying to escape into a strange dirt sky.
Aunt Erica swung the bird soundly across the block, stun-
ning it into stillness again. It looked very white against the
stained dark stump. For a moment her hand ax hovered

motionless above the thin, feathered neck, then thudded solidly down. The bird ran headless back in the direction of the chicken yard, as though now that its ordeal was over it wanted to return and have things just as they used to be. After several feet it folded into the long grass, trembling, kicking in a spastic little rhythm. Finally, only its blood-spoiled feathers quivered, as though stirred gently by some unseen breeze. The chicken yard had become calm again, the ancient racket of fear gone, the chosen hen forgotten. Aunt Erica hung the bird by its legs to let the blood drain. There did not seem to be very much blood, however. Maybe I just expected more than there was. What there was, was bright red. It dripped soaking into the dirt, absorbed darkly.

I watched also while the bird was plucked and cleaned and cut up. Then I watched as Aunt Erica put the pieces into a large paper bag of flour and seasoning, and shook them around until they were fully covered. I watched off and on as the pieces were fried. When the chicken dinner was served up that late afternoon, I ate a leg and a wing. As I ate them I tried to picture how they must have looked moving beneath the skin and feathers of the live chicken. As I thought over all that I had watched, I saw how everything fitted together. There was nothing sloppy about the whole thing. Later, I gathered some of the longer feathers, selecting only the most white and graceful, and I tried to make quill pens from them.

January 1949, contd.

Cynthia and I were supposed to share one of the downstairs bedrooms in Aunt Erica's house, which was a setup we both liked since we could take turns rubbing each other's backs before we went to sleep. Also, I could be with her when she cried at night. But the bedroom wasn't ready for our arrival.

"I wanted it ready in time," Aunt Erica said, "but labor is

just no count at all these days. Those niggers they sent over just piddled around and the paint hasn't gotten quite dry yet. So, Mary Jane, if this is all right with you, sweetie pie, we'll put Cynthia up with you for a couple of nights in your room and we'll let Speer stay over at Charlie's in Henry's room with him."

I told Ma that if she made me stay at Uncle Charlie's house with Henry, I would not let myself go to sleep. I told her that I would stay awake every night I was made to stay there. Ma suggested to Aunt Erica that the bed was large enough to hold the three of us easily and that we were all used to being bed partners. Aunt Erica said that it was about time I was growing up.

I did not want to take my shirt off in front of Henry because of my chest: because of the slightly sunken dip of the bones on its left side. Henry acted as though he didn't want to take his shirt off either. When he did I saw that his skin was white and quivery and wrinkled in little dimples like small cuts. I hurried and got my pajamas on, then I snickered at him.

"When I was six I was a lot bigger than you are," Henry said.

"I know lots of kids I'm bigger than," I told him.

"Sure. Little babies, I bet."

"Being big doesn't matter. It's how smart you are that counts. And I'm smart. I'm even almost as smart as Cynthia."

"Big deal."

I lay on my back as uncomfortable as possible. All the night, I told myself. I raised my legs up under the heavy covers, holding them rigid until they ached. I would never go to sleep.

"What are you doing, anyhow?" Henry asked. "How come you're holding your dumb legs up in the air?"

"Just because."

"Why?"

"None of your business."

"You get them down."

"You're not my boss."

"I can beat up anyone on this whole street. I can even beat up some niggers who are older than me. That's how come the kids call me Hercules. Because there was a movie here about him and he was real strong. He was the strongest man who ever lived."

"You don't have to tell me who Hercules was. Anyhow, so what? That's a dumb name. And Hercules was dumb too."

"Here's so what," Henry said.

He jabbed into my side under the covers.

The bedroom door was partially open and from the hallway, light leveled through the darkness to cross Hercules' face. He jabbed again deep into my side below my ribs, taking my breath away. He had made his point. I was no idiot. I dropped my dumb legs.

"Have you learned your lesson yet?"

"I'm going to tell."

"Is the little thing crying?"

"No, I'm not!"

"We'll see what we can do about that."

He jabbed into my side again.

"Why don't you try and hit me back?"

He jabbed again.

"That's just my ol' left. When it gets tired I use the ol' right."

"You quit it. I'll tell."

He jabbed again.

"Shut up, little baby, and take your medicine."

"Some day I'll kill you. When I grow up I'll get a knife and kill you if you don't quit."

He jabbed again.

"You're gonna learn your lesson, little baby, if it takes the whole livelong night," Hercules told me earnestly.

Holes.

Now, about Tarzan. About how his body arched as he dove from the high cliffs into the dangerous water below. Dangerous, deep water: a lake with no bottom, the natives said. For a very long time, Tarzan swims underwater, seemingly suspended in the fluid center of the screen. His eyes, bulging like a toad's, remain always open and on the alert. Like a strange water plant's blooming, his hair sways and sweeps about his head. When at last he surfaces, he is inside a cave, whose moist rock walls climb high out of sight into the darkness. Bracing his arms upon a ledge, Tarzan takes a well-deserved breather. It happens quickly, and with but a shudder of muscle he is pulled back into the water. Although he chops desperately at the groping tentacles, they slowly entangle him, pulling him deeper and deeper into the dark water toward the creature's huge glowing eyes. Unblinking eyes: yellow, luminous. And yet there is no hatred in those terrible eyes. And when Tarzan at last plunges toward them, there is no evident fear. And no evident pain as Tarzan's knife slashes them. And as inky foam spews from their wounds, those weird eyes give no sign of terror, or anger, or even regret.

She has blond, soft-looking hair. Her blue eyes seem almost too large for her beautiful, oval face. The creepy clay-people find her hiding out in the sunken forest, and since Flash is not there to defend her, she is captured easily. As she tries to twist free from their crumbly fingers, the long delicate muscles of her arms and legs flex. Her uniform, short to begin with, is ripped in several places during the struggle. Now, a large section of her midriff, her left shoulder, and the soft upper swelling of her left breast are bare. Deep in their hidden caves, the clay-people chain her to a pillar where, even as I watch, the damp soil begins to hungrily engulf her. Like the movement of mold over moist bread, the spongy clay will spread over her white flesh until she, too, will become a clay-person: featureless, mute, an earthen zombie.

Now, in our town there were two theaters: the Kayton and the Avalon. The beautiful, blond girl was being held captive in the Kayton, where in that strange limbo between serial reels, she was forced to await her predestined escape. But I did not get to see her escape. The weekend following the girl's capture at the Kayton, a Walt Disney feature was to start playing at the Avalon. Walt Disney features are good for kids; not only are they educational but they also stimulate a kid's imagination. Besides, as Ma pointed out, the blond girl would get free; blond girls always get free in the serials. But I knew this, and it had nothing to do with the whole thing. To see if she escaped or not had nothing to do with the reason I did not want to miss the serial. Instead, it was the very fact that the blond girl, frightened, helpless, was bound to that pillar as her flesh grew into earth. It was how she would struggle desperately to free herself. It was how her uniform was torn. It was the upper swelling of her left breast. It was how I would sit in the dark theater watching silently from a distance.

Holes, contd.

Years before I was born, my Great-Uncle Jarvis was unlucky enough to get his along with sixteen other men in a mine explosion. Because of the poisonous methane gas and because the explosion had ignited a fire in a deep coal seam, the rescue teams could not retrieve the bodies. Finally, the mine portals were sealed, and, as far as I know, have remained so for over forty years. As was often the case in such circumstances, smoke from the fire began pouring up out of the mine's ventilation holes. I have been told that my great-grandmother began rising at daybreak on each Sunday morning and walking to one of these smoke holes which was just over the ridge from her home. I am told that she would sit there through the whole morning talking down that thin column of smoke like it was some sort of weird telephone line to poor old Jarvis, her squashed son. For many years she did this. Finally they put the old girl away.

Coal is a fossil fuel. It was formed when millions of years ago the great Carboniferous forests settled slowly into their own marshes and folded themselves there into the dark inner layers of mountains. Many sorts of fossils can be found in the shale partings of coal seams. Even the casts of whole tree trunks and roots have been found in coal beds. Long ago, people thought that fossils were made by magic forces deep within the earth's heart that had failed somehow to breathe their creations to life. The ancient Greeks had the notion that petrified bones were the remains of dwarves and giants who had once roamed the earth. Later yet, in medieval Europe, fossils were thought to be the relics of saints or, on the contrary, the skeletons of drowned pre-Noahian sinners.

Because of Catherine, that wonderful drunken nut who was full of laughs, I was made aware of many of the above details when I was just a squirt. They fascinated me. The whole idea of petrification fascinated me. Somehow, in my weird-kid head, I associated it with what I knew about the intriguing subject of vampires and zombies, or any of the many other categories of living-dead with which I was acquainted via such dandy sources as Catherine, dear old Ma, and the best reading material a kid of my time could possibly get his hands on, namely the old E. C. comics, with all of the wonderfully gruesome horror of rotting corpses rising from graves to seek revenge upon the living, tales of terror brought to you by the Old Witch, the Vault Keeper, and my own favorite, the Crypt Keeper. Anyway, I recall that it occurred to me at the time that perhaps the clay-people could be considered as special zombies, as sort of mobile fossil forms, and that therefore the beautiful blond girl was in danger of becoming one also. And, also, Jarvis. Maybe one day someone would dig across his petrified bones. Bones which would somehow rise up into life again and move horribly among us. Or maybe someone, someday, would open a seam of shale and find him imprinted there like an ancient fern. Maybe he would even be used as fuel, his fingers burned like black tapers. Burning coal has a sweet decaying smell. Maybe, I thought, after a while all dead people smell like that, like burning coal. And on those days the coal smoke was particularly heavy from the Alloy Plant's coke ovens up the river, I thought that it must be like smelling the whole world dead.

"Did you see those soldiers give you the once-over?" my stupid fat Aunt Hilda asks my Ma.

"Don't be silly," Ma says.

"They were giving you the eye all right."

"Don't talk foolish."

"Well, I caught you checking your seams."

"For God's sake, Hilda!" Ma says, laughing. "You are so full of shit."

We are walking home from the movie at night. There is my beautiful Ma, my stupid fat Aunt Hilda, my rotten cousin, Henry, and my dying sister, Cynthia. My sister and Henry roam far ahead of the rest of us down the dark streets. Sometimes they hide behind hedges waiting for us to catch up; then they jump out yelling, hoping to scare the shit out of us. Then they run on ahead again.

I also go a little ahead of Ma and Aunt Hilda, but never far. Along the street side of the walk, there are trees spaced every five yards or so, and I run ahead from tree to tree, hiding within that strange dark the trees seem to shed like pools beneath them. As I run toward each tree, I try to titillate my fear by imagining that there are creatures back in the shadows, werewolves with quick wild eyes waiting to eat me raw. But it doesn't really work because at this particular time in my life I am not all that afraid of the dark. I hug tightly to

the tree's trunk and press my cheek against the rough bark.
I can smell the bark.

And, there, walking slowly toward where I wait in the
darkness, is my own beautiful dear old Ma. Over her face
the shadows of leaves move. Light from the streetlamp trims
her dark hair like a thin encircling flame. Now and then she
gives her head a slight toss and laughs softly and I can see
her teeth shining and the electric glow about her hair shim-
mer in the dark. She and Aunt Hilda approach. Holding
close in the shadows, I break like a low-down sneaky vampire
for the next tree. Quickly I am again at a tree's trunk, the
black core of the darkness.

Old Nero of burned Rome fame was apparently something of a card. I read somewhere that he examined his
murdered Ma's corpse with great relish, handling her legs
and arms critically, and, between drinks, discussing their
good and bad points. Also, for another laugh, he ordered her
womb torn open so that he could see where it had all started
out in the very beginning for him.

There is a shape and texture to darkness under trees. It
has a collapsed quality, a feeling of black space folding about
you. While I wait beneath that tree watching my beautiful
Ma walk toward me, my eyes are quick, wild. Maybe I am
dead after all. Maybe I am looking out from the darkness of
my own grave like a spook.

Boo.

Would you believe that I actually fell head over heels
into an open grave one time. I was stoned and juiced out of
my mind, of course. The breath was knocked out of me when
I hit the bottom and for a couple of moments I just lay there,
stunned, looking up at the wide bright rectangle above me
like it was some sort of strange movie of the sky. Then I
saw my own true love Mary (the girl I once almost, almost,
married). She had hurried to the grave's edge to peer apprehensively down in the darkness toward me, and, immediately

upon seeing her, my blooming head spun magically, crazily, with all sorts of dandy signs and symbols and sundry archetypes and I suddenly remembered vividly those walks home from the movies and looking out from under the dark trees at my dear old Ma coming toward me.

Two

Water safety.

On summer days Ma would often make a big pitcher of iced tea, and in that half-ass, haphazard way of hers would leave it sitting out somewhere in the kitchen instead of putting it away in the refrigerator. On my periodic treks through I would frequently hoist it up for a few quick gulps. On one particular day I spotted it sitting out on the stove and as usual I picked it up to drink. Eyes closed, head tilted far back, I gulped deeply. At first I thought that the object bouncing against my mouth was an ice cube, but then I realized that it was not cold. Apparently, the mouse had climbed over the back of the stove and had fallen into the tea, drowning. Later in the afternoon when two neighbor ladies stopped over for a brief visit with Ma, I offered to serve them up something refreshing to drink. Ma, delighted with my unusual display of manners, thanked me warmly.

Water safety, contd.

Once, a group of older boys, whose acceptance I wanted a great deal, decided to give me an initiation ordeal to see if I was brave enough to be a member of their gang. The plans for this ordeal were made up primarily by the gang's leader, a guy named Hutch, who because of his size and strength and guts was greatly admired and emulated. Now, in our neighborhood there was a conduit which was several hundred yards long, going under both a road and an elementary school playground. Although the creek this conduit served was usually shallow, its water deepened into a relatively strong, thigh-high current in the narrow tunnel. Also, the conduit bent in a continuous curve so that from within the tunnel the opening of either end could be seen for only about thirty feet. At first, my ordeal as determined by Hutch was simply to walk through this tunnel against the current. Later, he decided that to really test what sort of shit I was made of, I should be holding my cock out as I went through. And then, when we reached the conduit to begin the initiation, another touch was added. One of the guys had found a dead cat on the creek bank. It had already started to smell and its face was infested with small white worms. Of course, this was too good to be left out. Now, Hutch told me, I was to hold my cock out with one hand and with the other hand I was to carry the cat by the tail. If I dropped the cat I was supposed to stop and search around beneath the stinking water until I found it again. I couldn't leave the tunnel without it. I would fail the whole ordeal, Hutch told me, if I lost that damn cat. What's more, he said he would beat my ass if I lost that cat. So if I lost anything at all back in that tunnel, it had best be my puny cock, he warned me.

As I picked up the cat's body I tried to keep my hand from shaking too visibly. For a moment I thought I was about to puke, but I managed to swallow it back down. As we walked along the bank toward the conduit's entrance, Hutch dropped his heavy arm around my shoulder and reminded me again of all the sewers which emptied into this creek. And those small spongy things I would feel bouncing against my legs would be turds, he said. And those glowing beads I would see in the dark—those would be the insane eyes of starving rats: sewer rats, the largest, the most vicious kind of all. And I might as well expect to have my cock bitten, he told me. Because the tunnel was full of rabid fish and crawdads. As I entered the water the gang members started chunking rocks about my steps, shouting to me that they were tossing at snakes they could see slithering quickly toward my legs.

I know about a lot of things that have forsaken the light. Rats the size of cats roaming in herds throughout the deep caverns of forgotten New York City sewer lines. Infant alligators, Florida novelties, flushed into the darkness of those same sewers, to grow there, sunless, white as salt. Animals leaving by successive generations the outer world of light, moving passive and gentle into the deeper and deeper recesses of Kentucky caves, accommodated there below where not even bats fly. Noetoma, cave-rat, eyes large and lustrous, but blind in the midnight of Mammoth Cave. And the floating electric heads in the six-mile Tuscarora Deeps like Halloween jack-o'-lanterns, with mouths fanged like wolves, great staring eyes, bodies shredded ribbons of tissue. Deeps migrated into from the fertile tidal silts, the continental shoals, for refuge. And nothing grows down there, ever. And those creatures which have sunken there have only the waste, the dead bodies, that filter down slowly like a dead snow from the higher waters to feed and live upon.

Quickly, the light withers from about that kid, and I can't see him any longer. Everything returns to the memory of touch now. The pressing of the black water. The starved closeness of the dark. The hunched expectation of pain. Staggered often in the surging water, the kid falls painfully into the black wet walls. When his exposed cock starts to stiffen the kid is at first astounded. Then, confused, scared, he tries to stuff it to safety inside his pants. Distracted, he stumbles, falling forward into the stinking water. Its sourness strangles into his throat. He starts to puke. His blind eyes burn. He drops the damn cat.

Hutch and the other guys are gathered waiting about the tunnel's entrance, just shadows against the motionless light. They stand there looking back in the darkness toward where I wait pressed tightly against the wall. But they can't see me. I wait quietly, for the damn cat has been lost and so there is nothing more to do. I'm not going to go out there without it and get my ass kicked by that son-of-a-bitch Hutch, that's for sure. Since choking in that lousy water I have puked a couple more times, and still my belly tightens, constricts. But now, as I wait, I strangely feel all the danger of the darkness

and of the water lift from me. And the shape of the water
about my legs, the very motion of its smell and sound, and
the accommodation of the darkness, all of these things become recognized by me, and they come together to guard me.

For a long time Hutch and the gang wait, often chunking
rocks back into the darkness, some of these splashing near
me. But they are harmless. Hutch and the gang and the
rocks they chunk can't hurt me. And I just wait, quietly.
They start to call to me. They call to me that I am a dumb
shit. That I was stupid to fall for the ordeal bit. That they
would never let anyone in the gang who was dumb enough
to walk around in a dark sewer tunnel with his cock hanging
out. I am really a dumb shit all right, they call. They've sure
got a point about that, I think to myself. They start throwing
rocks again, and, sometimes, branches and old boards. After
several tries I manage to grab one of these branches as it
floats past me. It feels slimy.

"All right, dumb shit," Hutch calls to me. "All right, I'm
coming in after you. And buddy, your ass is grass and I'm
the mower. Do you hear that, turdhead? Your ass is as good
as kicked."

I move nearer to the wall, pressing my face against its
dampness, with its sour, old moss smell thick in my breath.
Hutch strikes a match, holds it in front of him, and steps
through the entrance. Slowly, he starts into the tunnel toward
where I wait. The small flame moves strange shadows up
over his face. When the match burns out he stops to strike
another. And another. So slowly, carefully, Hutch moves
deeper into my dark turf. I just wait, feeling strangely easy
and loose. Several times he stops to call threats to me, but
then always he keeps coming, for everyone is watching and
he is such a big brave shit.

I wait. I wait until he is directly in front of me, so near
that I can hear his breathing. When I slam into his face with
the branch, swinging it through the darkness like a ball-bat,

he screams just once before falling back into the smelly water where he starts splashing around wildly and crying like a goddamn girl.

Water safety, contd.

At night when I was a kid when I took my bath the warm water would make the knot swell in my left lower abdomen, just at the base of my cock. Watching for it became a comfortable ritual. I would just settle back in the water and wait for it to come, and I never had to wait very long. It would come sliding up slowly from some place behind my scrotum, or, rather, from behind what passed as my scrotum. Come sliding under my wet skin like some small live thing that was trying to swim up inside my body. Sometimes I would lie there and shut my eyes and try to picture it doing just that: swimming all the way up through the channels of my stomach and chest and throat until at last it reached my mouth. I would even try to imagine how it might taste. Then I would picture spitting the thing into my bath water, where, just as it hit the surface, it would become a small bright fish which would begin to flex and swim about my legs.

After a time, however, the knot would just stop swelling and I would rub my fingers around on my skin above it, rolling it around like a small stone under there. Sometimes when I would press on it with any pressure, my whole body would tingle with a feeling similar to that strange lift sensation you get when you are on an elevator which starts and stops too suddenly. Sometimes I would just lie there and try to order the thing to go back down where it had come from. Since it was a part of my own body, I told myself, I should be able to control what it did, where it went. It only seemed fair that I should be able to do this. I couldn't, of course.

When I was finished taking my bath I was supposed to call out so that someone could come in to look at me, to check my condition. This meant to finger around between my legs, poking and jabbing, and to have me turn my head to one side and cough. This was a real drag and since I never knew for sure who would be coming in any particular evening, I always held out for as long as possible before I called. I stretched everything out for as long as I could, often using up all the hot water in the house. The tub was a huge old-fashioned type, set up off the floor on large lion paws, and in the course of a nightly bath I would sometimes refill it several times, unplugging the stopper and at the same time running more hot water. After a while the air in that room would begin to feel like hot breath. The floor's white hexagonal tiles would become as slick as wet shells, as though they were being spread slowly over with some strange warm frost. And all the mirrors in the room would steam. And in the midst of it all I would float. I was suspended in all that warmth and it spread over me like sleep. I was a part of it. More than that even. I was its center. It went out from me.

By the time my skin, especially at my fingertips and toes, began to look like it had been carved with small, soft, bloodless cuts, someone would be banging on the door to tell me to get on the stick. Usually whoever knocked was the one who planned on looking me over that evening so at least I knew ahead of time who it would be. If it was someone I didn't mind that much, I would tell them to come on in and get it over with. Otherwise, I would stall for as much longer as I could. Of course, I minded everyone to some degree, only some not as much as others.

Aunt Erica, I guess, knew more than anyone what she was doing since she had at one time been a registered nurse. But, although she never hurt me, she always put rubbing alcohol on her hands when she touched me, and I didn't go for the cold, stinging way it felt. Also, it made the bathroom smell antiseptic like a doctor's office or like a hospital corridor and I didn't go for that either. And I was aware that you rubbed your hands with alcohol in order to clean them, and since Aunt Erica rubbed hers after she touched me as well as before, I sensed that she must have thought touching me like that was a pretty unsanitary thing to do, that what she touched was an unsanitary thing. And her face would always look strained, the flesh tight in a strange slick way, her expression frozen. Also, I remembered how she frequently reminded me to wash my hands well whenever I touched "it," like when I took a leak, so that I would not carry low-down, rotten germs to my mouth when I ate. I had a pretty good idea how Aunt Erica felt about "things" all right.

Ma, certainly, was acceptable; and she was very gentle. But I could tell that for some reason she didn't like to check me over and therefore I didn't much care for her doing it. Of everyone, Catherine was the best about it, although when she first started coming in to check me over she had long fingernails and sometimes they scratched me. She called those long nails her one concession to womanly wiles, and I knew that she had spent some time growing them and that she took pains to keep them filed and painted. Also, I recalled how irritated she was when on occasion she broke one. Therefore, because I liked the way in which she went about checking me and because I was afraid she would quit, I didn't say anything about the nails scratching me. She made me feel comfortable all right. She would make a big joke out of the whole thing. She would tickle me and ask me whose little "worm" that was and she would tell me to watch out for low-flying birds who might try to take a bite. But her nails hurt and finally one evening I inadvertently whined. Catherine cut them off that same night.

Of all my experiences with these goddamn examinations, the ones involving my stepfather were the worst. But these happened when I was a little older and therefore had more understanding about the situation. Also, he examined me on only a few occasions and since Ma was around each time, it was not as bad as it could have been; although even she could not prevent him from jerking me about and at least twice slapping me when, according to him, I was being uncooperative by not standing still enough or by flinching from his touch. His hands as much as his attitude bothered me. They were the largest of any I have ever seen and they looked brutal. The inner sides of several fingers were stained yellow from cigarette smoke, and his knuckles had deep grooves across them that looked like wicked cuts. They looked as though some power dangerous to me was held in them: a power which might at any time get loose. Of course, the bastard only examined me in the first place because of Ma, certainly not because of any genuine concern about my condition. A gesture to Ma, such as it was, to show how completely he had assumed all the burden of a prefabricated family.

When Mary and I first got together, we talked a lot about our respective pasts, which was something I had never done before with anyone. I found out too late I should have kept my mouth shut with Mary also. Unfortunately for me, she had a tendency to use what I had told her about myself as ammunition against me when we were fighting. Also, being a typical psychology major, she got a big kick out of analyzing everything to death, then popping off with unwelcome judgments. On one occasion she said that perhaps I was being unfair toward my stepfather. He had, after all, done the proverbial right thing concerning my Ma. And I should not forget, Mary said, that Ma had been a widow with two kids, both of them screwed up. One of them, in fact, was dying. I told Mary to shut her smirking face. I was not being unfair, and none of the things Mary said made any difference. There were things she simply did not understand, such as the way my dear old stepfather behaved about my condition and about Cynthia's illness, especially Cynthia's illness. The shame and resentment that he was not very successful in hiding. Shame because of Cynthia's appearance. Resentment because after a while he obviously no longer considered the full-time lease to Ma's beautiful body worth the burdens he had inherited. And, although everyone thought he was some kind of hot shit hero, with his war wounds and all, he wasn't really. He was just another chickenshit, that's all.

Fish stories.
I read that in 1530 the herring vanished from the sea around Heligoland. Local fishermen attributed this to the actions of two boys who had beaten a freshly caught herring and then had tossed it, broken and suffering, back into the sea.

The Kwakiutl Indians of British Columbia take care to throw salmon bones and offal back into the sea in order that the fish's soul may reanimate them at the resurrection of the salmon. If these bones were burned, the fish's soul would be forever lost and the salmon could not rise from the dead.

Also, in British Columbia, if fish fail to come in their season, a Nootka wizard fashions an image of a swimming fish and then positions it in the water in the direction from which the fish usually appear. Accompanied by a special prayer this ceremony will force the fish to arrive shortly.

The Egyptian priests hated the sea, calling it the foam of Typhon. Not only were they forbidden to place salt on their tables but also they refused to converse with pilots or fishers. Of course, they would not eat fish. The hieroglyphic symbol for hatred was a fish.

A July, I think. I am walking with someone onto the Ritter Street bridge. I am not sure who I am with. Maybe I am with my Grandpaw or my Uncle Charlie. I am being lifted up to the metal railing to look down at the dead fish in piles all around the river bank. Some are floating up on their sides at the water's edge, their eyes wide open as if they are looking into the sky. The stink of rot rises in the hot air even as high as the bridge. Colored garbagemen, handkerchiefs tied over their lower faces, are shoveling the dead fish into the bed of a truck backed down onto the dark sand. Someone standing near me says that poison did it; that's what did it. Poison from the Alloy Plant killed all the fish. And poison from the strip mines up the river.

In 1939, a Middlesex University sophomore swallowed sixty-nine live goldfish, becoming the champion in this activity.

Because they eat garbage and therefore begin to stink soon after death, carp are usually kept alive for as long as possible in tanks in the rear of the fishmarket. This was what I told my true love Mary once, when we happened to stop in front of a fishmarket's window. We had been walking randomly about the streets near the campus for several hours. Of course, we had been fighting. When I told her this about the fish she said that that was as good reason as any to be kept living. We stood there for a while in front of the window, just silently looking in at the bins of crushed ice which were stuffed full with fish. With perch, flounder, mullet, mackerel: all arrested, arched in a frozen swim to nowhere. From their faded scales and from the stained ice, steam rose like some strange cold smoke to haze the lower glass. After a time, Mary told me that I was something of a cold fish myself. As cold and frozen sometimes as any of those fish in the bins. I told her that long ago the Egyptian hieroglyphic symbol for hatred had been the fish.

The making of men.

They told me that it was the largest private hospital in the whole world and that kids came from all over to be treated there. Therefore, I would probably meet some interesting kids. Maybe even some from foreign lands. I wasn't going there just to get carved. I was going there to broaden my cultural experience.

I was put in a semiprivate room with a red-headed kid who was a bleeder. If he spent too much time on his feet, they would swell and turn black. Since the same thing happened to his knees if he crawled, the red-headed kid did not get around much. They said that if he ever cut himself, he might not be able to stop bleeding. Because of this he could never play or anything like that. He cried a great deal and this got on my nerves. His old lady was always hanging around and he would whine continuously to her. Also, he would call her names. He told her that she was stupid and smelly and fat. She sat in a chair at the end of his bed and just smiled all the time. Naturally, I hated that kid and his lousy red hair with all of my heart. I told him once that some night when he was sound asleep I planned to sneak over and stick him with pins. When I told him this he started to blubber which made me giggle and snicker like crazy.

I had dreams about him after he was finally carted away to an intensive care room. I dreamed that I actually did stick him with a pin and that he exploded. It was something like popping a blood-stuffed tick. And blood sprayed all over the room, making unusual dark whorled patterns on the walls and ceiling. And his skin wrinkled up, shrinking like the rubber of a pierced white balloon. And, also, like a balloon quickly deflating, his skin whizzed about through the air near my head as though it was after me for revenge. And I was scared shitless of it. And I ran frantically around the room trying to escape it. And all this time his old lady was chasing the whizzing skin while it was chasing me. And she was laughing crazily, even as she bounced and fell against the walls and furniture.

The same morning the kid with red hair was carted away, I was given a new roommate, a boy younger than myself, probably seven or eight. He had been involved in a freak accident in which a high-power line had fallen across his body, nearly electrocuting him. He was scarred severely from his left shoulder across his chest and stomach to his crotch. His genitals had been burned away. Because he had been receiving skin grafts for several years, he was well known by the hospital personnel, many of whom visited him frequently. For those visitors he seemed to know and like especially well, he had a surprise which he would show them with great enthusiasm. Literally beaming with pride the kid would draw aside his covers and lift his gown to show them. Apparently, someone who loved him had told him that the small mutant slab of skin which had begun to grow between his legs was a brand-new prick. All the time he was in the room with me, I never heard anyone tell him any differently. Finally, I had to clue the kid in myself.

My next roommate was a hero. He was around fifteen but looked older. He had had his legs run over while pushing another kid from the path of a truck. He was handsome and he laughed a great deal. The nurses all really liked him. And many different nuns came around to visit him. They told him that he was brave and that God would bless him. A young priest came in several times to talk with him. The priest told him that he was brave and that God would bless him. He was not to lose faith, the priest told him. After the hero's legs were chopped off, he was told by the priest and the nuns that God would surely help him. He replied to them that he had faith in God and in God's help.

I asked him how it felt to have his legs gone. He said that he could still feel them, and, in fact, there was often pain coming from where they had been. Sometimes, he said, he would wake up at night and forget for a moment that they were gone.

"I guess it'll slow up my ballgame," he said, and laughed.

But he was not going to let it get him down. He thought that he might like to be a priest someday. Or a doctor, maybe.

Some calling in which he would be able to help others as others had helped him.

I told him that he made me sick to my stomach and that I thought that he was probably the dumbest shit I had ever known.

The making of men, contd.

A brief portrait of my junior high school gym coach. A short man, heavy and bald, with a flattened nose. Small unblinking eyes that "never miss a trick so no use trying to pull the wool over them." Played second string on a country high school football team. Cut in his freshman year from a small state college football roster but hung on as an assistant manager for the track team. Unmarried. Drove an old Ford with a huge pair of purple parafoam dice dangling from the rearview mirror. Always wore white socks with colored stripes at their tops, even with suits. In other words, a near perfect archetype. His philosophy: a man has to have two things to be both a man and a gentleman. One, intestinal fortitude. Two, body cleanliness. In regard to the latter, he had signs up all over the gym dressing room warning you to take your shower after class or else, and warning you to follow the safety rules while you were taking your shower or else.

Now, Charlie Wilks. Big bad Charlie Wilks. Rangy farm buck. School bus rural.

"No nut   No nut   No nut."

He was not saying it all that loudly. Simply pointing at me and saying it over and over. Others gathered around. I kept my back to them and continued to dress. By this time I had my undershorts on.

"No nut   No nut   No nut."

He was standing there naked, wet from the shower. He started flipping his towel at the bare backs of my legs. Everything else had grown still. Sounds only of his words, of the towel snapping expertly through the air. I had on my shirt. I bent slightly, hopped to one foot to pull on a leg of my corduroy trousers. The shove was a light one, a mere pressure of fingers. But off-balance, the tile floor slick, still barefoot. I rolled over as quickly as possible trying to complete pulling on my pants. Those pants had to get the hell on, fast. Everyone was laughing now. I could feel the wet soaking up into my shorts from the floor. From ear to ear I made with the old shit-eating grin. Good sport. Could take it with the best of them.

"What's going on here? What the hell's bells going on in here?"

Enter Coach with paddle: two feet long, handle wrapped in green tape, quarter-inch holes in parallel lines down its surface.

"He didn't take no shower," Charlie Wilks said pointing to me.

"Yeah, he never does," someone else said.

"Yeah, he never does," others offered.

"What's all this all about?" Coach asks me.

I could not quite pull the pants on. One of the legs had knotted. Coach stood directly over me.

"You hear me, mister? Something wrong with your ears, mister?"

"No."

"No what?"

"My ears are all right."

"Well, mister, you answer me pronto when I ask you a question. Now what about this here shower business? You been duckin' the showers or something? You been trying to pull the wool over my eyes, mister?"

"No."

"No what, mister?"

"I'm not pulling wool. Or anything."

"You been taking your showers like you should or not?"

"Yes."

"No he hadn't no he hadn't," everyone in chorus.

"Woe to your ass, mister, if you're lying to me. Now have you or not been taking your showers?"

"No."

"You got a legitimate reason?"

"He ain't got no nuts," Charlie Wilks offered.

"What's that?"

"Nuts," Charlie Wilks said again. "He ain't got any."

"You got a disability, mister?" the coach asks me.

"Sort of."

"What does that mean? Look, either you got one or you don't."

"All right, I got one."

"Name it."

"Undescended testicles. I mean, I got them, they're just not all the way down is all."

"That's better. Isn't that better to get it out in the open? Get it off your chest. One thing you gotta learn in this man's world is that it's tough; it's dog eat dog. You gotta have the intestinal fortitude to stand up to the hard knocks. Life is no bed of roses. Life is one hard row to hoe. Gotta face up like a man. Now, this just don't go for what's his name here. This goes for all you guys. You don't get rid of problems by hiding from them. Now, you get up off your tailbone, mister. You strip yourself down. Right now, mister. Get a move on."

When I had stripped down, Coach told me to turn around and face everyone. He told me to walk out to the middle of the dressing room. He told me that since I had been cutting showers I had something coming. I had broken the rules, he said, and this was to be an example for everyone.

"Make an ass, mister."

I bent over. I had five big ones coming, he said. As was the custom, everyone counted out loud with the strokes. Because I flinched upright with two of the strokes, two more were added.

Later, when I thought over what had happened, I recognized that there was nothing sloppy about what the coach had done. It was a precise exercise of his power, and there was a sort of weird cleanness about it. In essence, he had manipulated me through a series of affirmative motions: affirmative of his situation, his reality. It was a necessary action for him. Just as my subsequent actions were necessary for me. I started off by cutting his car's tires. Later, I put sugar in his gas tank. Then other things. For several years I vandalized his property at least once every term. But this was not completely a personal thing; this was not revenge in the strictest sense. Rather, it was a process of discovery for me about my own situation, about my own boundaries: to see how far I would be willing to go, to see what manner of risks I would take as I colonized my turf and made it safe for only me.

And old Charlie Wilks got his, too. Got it one mild autumn evening after a football game. Got it in a deadend alley two blocks from the stadium, with quite a number of kids standing around watching and cheering us on. And this time the laughs weren't on me.

Beside a lake.

I worked one summer in the coke plant of Republic Steel in Cleveland, Ohio. The working conditions in this part of the plant were lousy, with a lot of smoke and grime, and with a strong radiant-heat hazard. Except for the shift foremen, who were usually Polish, the workers were blacks. In fact, besides myself, there were only a handful of other white men in the whole labor force, and these were primarily college students like myself, hired for summer jobs. This was a strange point of pride with many of the blacks, especially among the older ones, as they seemed to think that white men were not up to such work.

I met one young black, however, who did not feel the same way about the job at all. He was in his early twenties, had attended a community college for a year, had served in the marines for four years, and had just before his recent discharge returned from combat duty in Nam, where he had been twice decorated. In his opinion, the job in the coke plant sucked. I agreed wholeheartedly with him about this, and also about many other things, as I was to find out. Since we worked on the same shift rotation and on the same furnace battery, we talked quite a lot, sharing our stocks of Polish jokes. After a time we became friends and started to spend many of our off-hours together, making the scenes in Black Cleveland, where he really knew his way around. The dude's name was Finus.

Since we were both going to get off over the long July 4th weekend, Finus suggested that we hit a small resort town on the lake northeast of Cleveland, where there was usually some action. This is just what we did.

The girl, although somewhat thin, was good-looking, with close-cropped blond hair, a nice smile, and very large, watery, blue eyes. How she came to be with us I don't remember; and I can't remember her name. I do recall, however, that she was a sophomore prelaw major from Ohio University, and that although she was always partially drunk or stoned while with us, she was obviously quite intelligent. She proved to be not only a sweet chick with no bullshit jive but also to be very funny company. She was more or less engaged, she said, but was not going to let that fact cramp her style.

Throughout the day of the 4th, the three of us wandered rather aimlessly from bar to bar along the town's main street. The bars, the sidewalks, and the streets were packed with milling crowds of people, mostly young college plastic-hip types. Except for a joint now and then, we concentrated mostly on boozing. I went through several drunk-sober cycles

and by the late afternoon I was tired to the verge of sickness.
The others said they felt fucked up too. We realized that we
had not eaten during the day and decided that if we did we
would feel better. From a small grocery store we bought food
which we could get together ourselves, including a small
sack of potatoes and a box of tin foil in which to bake them.
We then took off among the rolling dunes of the expansive
beach, hunting for a place where we could build a fire and
could eat and hang out with privacy.

"Are you really going to let him do this?" the chick asked
me, and although she was trying to hold her voice together,
it was trembling slightly.

I could feel her eyes from across the low flames trying
to fasten themselves to mine, trying to claim some sort of
bullshit allegiance I guess. I didn't say anything back to her.
I just sat there looking into the fluted shadows of the fire. I
was really not all that much in favor of what was going to
happen to her, but I wasn't going to get messed up with it.
Besides, I could dig why Finus had to do it.

Once again, filled with anger this time:

"Are you actually going to just sit there on your ass and
let him get away with this?"

I still didn't say anything. What the shit, she was making
too big a thing out of it. I just sat there digging the fire.

She was quick and graceful with her fear, I'll say that.
But old Finus was quicker, and he clutched her hand as she
swirled toward the dark to run. He flicked his fist into her
lower stomach. She fell down and rolled childlike around
the core of her pain. She moaned faintly. Finus slowly turned
around from her and squatted again within the failing glow
of the fire's circle. Shimmering prismatic points of sweat
covered his face. His eyes, though, didn't look all that excited
or eager, but just stared quietly, evenly, into the flames.

After a time she quit moaning. Then, very quietly, almost

tenderly, Finus told her that she would not be hurt again if she did what he told her to do. He got up and walked over to her. Slowly, very deliberately, he unbuttoned her denim shirt. She rose to her elbows when he started to slip it from her shoulders. When he started sliding down her jeans she arched her narrow hips upward.

I lit a joint, then got up and walked off toward the water. The small surf settled, broke calmly into phosphorescent foam along the black beach. Out along the curve of the night lake, the lights from the towns were gathered like low constellations, and as I stood there on the shore getting good and stoned, I traced imaginary lines among various of them. I gave them the names of weird animals and then made up strange legends about how these animals had become fixed along the shore in patterns of lights. This was something I had often done before when looking out across clusters of lights at night. I could kill a shitpot of time doing this. Over the years I had even formulated secret signs and symbols for my weird zodiac. But then this was one of my major pastimes: the arbitrary making of signs and symbols, the abstraction or reduction of things into symbols that could then be handled more easily.

I don't know how long I had been hanging out there when I heard something to my right a little ways up the beach. All I could see through the darkness was a blurred white form as it ran toward the lake. I watched the form as it ran splashing into the water, then after a couple of moments I lost sight of it. I walked on down toward where it had entered the lake but I still couldn't see anything. After a while, Finus came walking down the beach toward me. He asked me if I had seen anything of the chick. I told him that I saw her hit the water a few minutes ago. At least I guessed that it was the chick, I told him.

"That was a pretty dumb fucken thing for her to do," Finus said. He lit up a joint, took a few drags, then passed it to me.

I told Finus that I agreed wholeheartedly with him. It was a pretty dumb thing all right to swim out in the lake alone at night. I told him that I had earned my senior life-saver's credentials at the Y.M.C.A. before I was fifteen and so I knew what I was talking about when it came to things like water safety.

Beside another lake.

It was June and very hot. I convinced Mary that what we needed to do to try to get things together again was to find a place where we could be private and naked and lazy. I rented a small cabin by a lake which was near enough to the city and the campus so that we could come in without any trouble as often as we wanted. But I made Mary promise not to tip off any of her many friends where we were going to be.

The cabin was built of log and stone, and because of the deep shade of many nearby trees, it remained cool inside throughout the day. At night we slept on mattresses we pulled out onto the screened-in front porch. Most afternoons I spent working rather leisurely on my thesis, but during the mornings Mary and I hung out a lot on a nearby beach. Mary soon became very tanned, and her light brown hair, which she wore straight and long, began to streak blond from the sun. Her pregnancy had not started to show yet and because she was slender with very long, pretty legs, she looked great in her deep-red bikini.

During the mornings we spent on the beach we would frequently swim out to a raft that was secured several hundred yards from shore and spend relatively isolated hours there, diving, floating around, or just lying in the sun. The warm air and water would draw a moist, faintly salt taste to Mary's skin, a taste which would last throughout the day. And at night, hours since we had been in the sun, her flesh would still hold a sunlight fragrance and warmth. And often, very late at night, we swam in the deserted lake. We would get nice and high and then go out and float naked on inner tubes in the moonlight. We even started balling again.

Because we were usually up quite early, we often had the beach to ourselves in the mornings, and while waiting for the water to warm up a bit we started passing time by building elaborate sand constructions. Then, later, when people started arriving we would bet on which ones we thought looked like sand castle destroyers: ones who would not be able to resist sinking a foot into a finely shaped tower wall. I was correct much more often than Mary. In fact, there were times when I could predictably describe just how my selected destroyer would go about it: how deliberate or cautious or blatant or joyous or embarrassed he or she would be about it.

As I said, most afternoons I spent at the cabin where it was cool so that I could get in a little work on my thesis. Mary, however, usually stayed at the beach to work on her tan. One afternoon I just couldn't get the old gear creaking. Everything distracted me. Having tried to concentrate on my work for over two hours with little success, I just said screw it and I opened a cold, beaded can of beer which I guzzled down. After a couple more beers and a joint, I put on my trunks and headed down the path through the pines to the beach. When I got there I looked all around for Mary but she was nowhere to be seen. I went back up the beach to some rocks where the path from our cabin came out of the trees and I sat down in the shade. I sat there for a long time. Finally Mary and her new friend came out of the woods far down the beach. I didn't stick around. I went back to the cabin and got blasted in the proper way.

The next morning we went down to the beach early as usual. We didn't have a hell of a lot to say to each other. I just sat there in the morning sun, drinking beers from an ice chest. For a time Mary just sat there too, pretending to be greatly interested in a small scab on her knee which she kept picking at. Finally she started messing around in the sand as though she was going to build something. She was, all right. She found a branch half-buried in the sand, which she pulled loose and then with a big effort stabbed one end back in so that it stood erect. Then, while I just watched on, Mary took great pains in molding and shaping an enormous cock from the damp sand. It looked vaguely familiar, being somewhat bent out of shape and angling slightly to the left. On the head she did a truly excellent job. The pubic hair unfortunately was green, consisting of several handfuls of grass she found higher up on the bank. Of course, with her usual gentleness, Mary neglected the nuts.

When she finished she came over and flopped down beside me like she was really wasted from her labor of love. She asked me what I thought about her art work. I told her to fuck off. People started to show up soon. Mary began to chatter about who she thought looked like the probable sand sculpture destroyer. I tried not to pay any attention to her jive. I just sat there putting away the swill. Finally Mary selected a small blond girl of nine or ten as the destroyer. And it looked like she might be right for a change. Instantly upon spotting the strange pillar at the water's edge, the blond girl charged screaming toward it. But then, just as she descended upon it, she halted abruptly, digging her feet deep into the sand to brake her run. Then, quiet, motionless, she just stood there looking at it. Mary started giggling, putting her hand over her mouth to hide it like a kid. Soon, other children started to gather around the pillar and they also just stood silently in wonder. None of them made even the slightest gesture to touch the shaft, which by now was beginning to dry and to crumble slowly.

After a time, two women, apparently suspicious because of the silent group of children, approached to investigate. With some difficulty they waded through the small bodies toward the transfixing center. One moment only for recognition, shock, fear. Quickly, one woman began trying to disperse the kids, threatening them, slapping at them. The other woman with several hesitant half-kicks toppled the column's upper part. Then, impossible to hold back, the kids shrieking with happy laughter swarmed kicking and stomping upon the remnants of Mary's art, until, soon, the spot was churned into a slight depression of dark sand.

Three

July 1949.

The run-over dog, a brown and black bitch, was dying the whole morning. Wet gurgling sounds came from deep inside its body, and its tongue curled from its mouth, spreading flat and sticking onto the hot street bricks. Flies buzzed down about its head. They seemed to suck on its open eyes. They walked in and out of its mouth. More than all of this, though, were the puppies. Or what would have been puppies. Spilled among the blood and moist insides crushed from the dog's lower body. Tissue a bluish film over their furless bodies. Small rat bodies, with swollen heads, faces wrinkled, crunched inward. Stump limbs folded close across their fronts. Flies walked all over them also. We watched while the dog's eyes milked over dead.

We sat back on the curb in the shade, picking sweet grass blades from around the tree's roots to chew and suck. Cynthia got up from the curb and brushed her hand over her red shorts' seat. She spit out the grass blade and looked at Hercules and me, shaking her head.

"I best check it out again," she said.

She walked slowly over to the run-over dog, then waved her hands in the air over it to scatter the flies. She bent down, peering closely into its face. Blood was running from its mouth and was drying on the bricks. When it lifted its head toward Cynthia's close face, the dried blood strings from the corners of its mouth stretched like thin ropes of gum. Then its head fell quickly back onto the bricks again. Cynthia stood erect and walked back to the curb.

We talked in whispers for some reason.

"Is she almost dead yet?" Hercules asked.

"I think so."

"Are the little puppies dead yet?" I asked.

"They never were even alive," Cynthia said. "They hadn't been born yet."

"Were they dead before they were born?"

"Not exactly. They just weren't all the way alive yet."

"I saw the car what did it," Hercules said, telling us for the fifth time. "It was a two-door Ford convertible. A woman was driving."

"We should pull the miserable thing in closer to the curb out of the hot sun," Cynthia said.

"Sure, you go ahead and touch it and get rabies or something," Hercules said.

"Don't be so stupid," Cynthia told him. "Where in the shit do you get all of those simple ideas of yours? You're such a chickenshit!"

"Well, I know what I know. So you just go ahead and touch it then and get disease and stuff. See if I care."

Aunt Erica saw us. She came off her front porch and walked down to the street where we were sitting.

"Just what do you children think you're doing? Why, you-all just get the dickens away from here. Who knows what this old thing carried! Now youall get away!"

"See!" Herky smirked. "I told you all about disease. Cynthia was wanting to go pull on it, Aunt Erica."

"Well, I'm not surprised. It's a fine howdy-do. I just swand!"

"I just wanted to pull it in out of the sun," Cynthia said. She made a fist at Hercules behind Aunt Erica's back.

"Well, I don't care what you were settin' to do," Aunt Erica said. "Now, I said once for you all to get. Now get."

"It's my own body," Cynthia said. "So even if it is true about getting disease, it happens to be my own business if I get it or not."

"Now, you just watch your sassy mouth," Aunt Erica said. "You can sass everyone else around here and get away with it but not me, little girl! Now youall get away from this

old thing right now! I'm going right in to call the garbagemen to come get this old thing and you kids just stay completely clear of it!"

We stayed back up in the yard until we saw the big
rumbling yellow truck. The fat, colored garbageman was the
one. A red handkerchief was tied around his head and he
jumped down off the back of the truck with a long-handled
shovel. He crammed the wide blade under the dog's middle,
scooping it up. Its head and long tongue and legs swung
limply. The insides, the unborn puppies, were a reddish puddle dripping from the square end of the shovel. The flies
were still in a hovering swarm about the dog's face. Through
the thick leaves of the maples along the street, mottles of
sunlight and shadow moved softly over the bricks and over
Cynthia's hair in golden colors. The brown of the dog's fur
was golden also in the splashes of sunlight.

With a quick-jerk motion the man flung the dog up over
his shoulders,—Heave ho,

high into the bright air, the flies buzzing away in
scatters. Then, a bounceless thud from deep in the truck's
steaming dark bed. The black hungry flies settled back down
again onto the spots and the small meat smears and the yet
steaming splash of urine. They sparkled in the flushed shifting light like fluttering specks of tinsel.

Aunt Erica came back out and told us to get away again.
She connected up her garden hose and started washing the
bricks clean, the splash of water flowing brown into the
slant of gutter.

Babies.
It had been wrapped up in old newspaper, stuffed into a
shoebox, and the box then tied with heavy binding cord. One
of the garbagemen said that he remembered the box because
of the unusually secure way it was bound. He could not remember, however, exactly where they had picked it up. Prob-

ably in the fourth or fifth block of Elm Street. He had only noticed it at all by accident, when it had fallen free as a can was being hoisted to the truck's bed. He had picked the box up himself and had tossed it into the truck. In fact, he had a fleeting notion to take a look inside.

Several boys hunting with their pellet guns for rats in the town dump the following day next came across it. The box had been almost chewed completely away by rats. At first the boys were not sure of what they saw, since it had been partially eaten. The county coroner said that it had probably died of suffocation. In fact, it had possibly been very much alive and quite healthy when first placed in the can, although only a few hours old. The town newspaper observed that since Elm Street was in the best section of Century, whoever put the box in the can probably came from elsewhere.

I read once that among the Mbaya Indians of South America the women would destroy all their children except the one they believed to be the last. Any children born after this chosen one were murdered also. This practice eventually depleted a branch of the Mbaya nation, who had been for many years the most formidable enemies of the Spaniards.

Among the Lengua Indians of the Gran Chaco, the missionaries discovered what they described as a carefully planned system of racial suicide, by the practice of infanticide, by abortion, and by other methods.

The Jagas, a conquering tribe in Angola, are reported to have put to death all their children, without exception, in order that the women might not be encumbered with babies on the march. They recruited their numbers by adopting boys and girls of thirteen or fourteen years of age, whose parents they had killed and eaten.

A news article reported that a warrant had been issued by the F.B.I. for a twenty-year-old Wac, charging her with murder in connection with the death of a baby found wrapped in a blanket and stuffed in her wall locker. Authorities said that Spec. 5 Helen W. Bunch had departed the Ft. Bragg military installation June 15 on a thirty-day leave and had not been seen since that time. The body of the baby was so badly decomposed that neither the age nor the sex could be determined. It was discovered in the Wac's barracks June 19, when Miss Bunch's roommate returned from her leave and noticed a strong odor in the room.

The McCullers were such a nice young Christian couple, Aunt Erica said. And it was a pity that their very first baby was born with water on its brain. But God's ways are ways of mystery, she said. When we went to visit them one Sunday afternoon, I was told not to act as though anything was wrong and not to ask questions about the baby.

It was in a buggy in their living room. Mr. McCuller was humming and rolling the buggy back and forth gently over the edge of a rug. The baby's head was swollen double its normal size. It was hairless and the tight skin of the skull looked slick and glistened with bluish highlights. For a time after we arrived the baby was asleep, but then it awoke and started to cry. Mr. McCuller rubbed and patted its stomach until it was still again. Mrs. McCuller sat on a couch beside Aunt Erica. She talked and smiled continuously, smiling always with the same same strange smile: lips stretched and thin, teeth very white and large. Mr. McCuller rolled the buggy from the room. Soon later, he appeared in the doorway to say that he was going after cigarettes and would be directly back. Mrs. McCuller just smiled and continued talking.

Since she continued smiling and talking, I thought that she probably had not heard the baby. Anyway, at first it was not really crying, just making gurgling noises. All little babies do that, I told myself. Mrs. McCuller smiled and talked. And even the baby's crying at first was not very loud. But then it became loud, then louder. Soon it was choked on its sobs. Just as Aunt Erica got up and started for the bedroom, Mr. McCuller returned. As he hurried toward the sounds he paused at the doorway. Mrs. McCuller turned her smiling face toward him. A short time later we left. Mrs. McCuller walked with us out to the porch, and as we drove away, she smiled and waved to us.

The baby in the jar.

"You have to be practical to get through life," Aunt Erica always said. "If you're not practical you can't make do with a thing. And I always say that there is a blessing of God about practical ways of doing things."

For instance, according to Aunt Erica, the rows and rows of jars with the dead little beings suspended in the alcohol that her brother Alfonso, the Doctor, had collected when he was alive. His Grand Scientific Specimen Collection he had called them. And he was some collector he was, Aunt Erica told. What he could see in keeping all those dead things around she would never know. When you would hold the jars up and tilt them, the dead little things would bounce against the sides as though they were trying to push out, their skin or fur smudging against the bright glass, the light flickering and glancing through the murky liquid. He kept them in the attic and, needless to say, she told, they made the whole upstairs reek like a funeral parlor. Stunk to high heavens. Those specimens were a running argument between Aunt Erica and the Doctor for years, until finally one day when he was out on calls down Two Creek way and wouldn't be home until late, she had simply built a large trash fire out behind the house and had spent the whole morning sloshing those dead little things onto it. They had crackled and snapped like a pine cone fire, she told. And she had emptied every jar except one: the one with the mummified fetus, which was just an awful-looking thing, she said, with

its head all swollen and sour-cream colored. She had hidden
it away in the rafters of the attic, not to save it though, not
that, but because tossing such a thing out to burn on the
fire seemed too near like defiling a grave, she said. Even if
the grave was but a two-quart mason jar of alcohol.

Then she had boiled out the jars and had eventually set
up preserves and jellies in them. Now that was being practical, she said. That was making do with something in a
functional manner.

We looked all one morning but we couldn't find it.
Cynthia started at one end of the attic and I started at the
other. Rain thudded above us on the tin roof and swept in
against the high narrow windows. A single naked bulb swung
circling slowly, its light uneven, dim, moving shadows across
the trunks and boxes and old furniture. It had rained all
the night before and so we hadn't been allowed outdoors to
play, and after Cynthia had won her sixth straight game of
Chinese checkers from me, she said:

"Let's go find that dead baby in the attic. The one in the
bottle."

Listen, I had had bad dreams about that baby ever since
I first heard of it. And when at night I heard strange noises
from that spooky attic, noises, I was sure, like small feet
slapping across the board floors, I knew as sure as hell that
that baby was haunting around up there. That somehow it
had broken free from its bottle tomb and now stumbled blind
and dripping about the dark attic, its green swollen head
bumping painfully against the legs of old tables: soft,
stunted hands groping before it, feeling, touching.

You can bet I didn't search my end of the attic very well
that morning. I didn't go back in the deeper corners or look
in the dark behind things. I merely stood at the edges of the
light and watched the shadows move. I knew that I had no
business back in the dark, that I was at a disadvantage to
whatever lived back in there.

Catherine once spent the evenings of a whole month reading to Cynthia and me from Poe's tales of horror. When she read those collected accounts of people buried by mistake alive, how they awoke in the dark grave, realized suddenly that they were beneath the ground, were forgotten among the dead, how often they must have screamed themselves insane, I thought then of the dead baby in our attic. What if it did suddenly wake up? Would it scream? Could it scream?

For a time when I was a kid I had a weird image of heaven as being like an attic. Whenever someone would happen to mention "heaven," I would immediately picture old boxes tied with brown string, broken furniture, dust, dark corners, grimy windows, the smell of mildew and mothballs. I believe this was because of the word "save." I had heard that souls went to heaven to be saved, but what were souls and what was heaven? I knew also that things were saved up in the attic, that that was exactly what an attic was for, and these were things I could picture because I had seen them. They were real.

Although I was later led to believe that heaven was a swell joint to go to, that it had long golden streets, angels with harps, generally good weather, I always felt an initial tinge of distaste whenever it was mentioned. For a time I kept having a picture of my soul as a box tied with brown cord. Then later, I kept imagining my soul waking up in heaven only to find itself a sour-cream colored baby in a bottle in somebody's attic.

"What would you do with it even if you found it?" Catherine asked Cynthia.

"Who knows," Cynthia said. "Just look at it. Maybe we'd bury it out back in the yard."

"Well, I'm afraid I haven't the slightest idea where it is. I could never find it myself."

"You mean you looked for it too?"

"Indeedy I did. Don't you think I'd be well aware of the

grand spook possibilities of having a nice pseudo-corpse in one's attic?"

"A what?"

"A creepy cadaver."

"What's that?"

"Oh, just a dead body, of sorts."

"And you say you never found it either?"

"Nope. Never did. Never ever."

"Where all did you look?"

"Just about everywhere, I guess. I sleuthed that attic from crevice to cranny. Found other things though."

"What other things?"

"Oh, all varieties of things. An attic is a graveyard for a lot more things than babies in bottles. You just keep looking around. You might be surprised at what you can come across."

"Well, what were *you* going to do with that baby if *you* found it?"

"Well, I thought of several possibilities. I thought I might dress it up in dolly clothes and play house with it. Or I might just have wrapped it up all snug in blankets and maybe put it in a basket and then left it on the church steps. With a note attached, of course. Requesting that the foundling be raised up as a God-fearing Christian."

Babies, contd.

Among the Maoris, when a child's navel-string finally drops off, he is carried to a priest for a naming ceremony. But before the ceremony can actually begin, the navel-string must be buried in a sacred place and a young sapling must be planted over it. For then on, the tree, as it grew, was a *tohu oranga*, or sign of life, for the child.

In Ceram the child sometimes wears the navel-string around its neck as an amulet. In the islands of Leti, Moa, and

Lakor, a man saves his navel-string so that he may carry it as a talisman into battle or on a far journey.

Ma took my hand and pressed it gently against her swollen belly. We both waited very quietly. Her smile, as I think of it now, was beautifully conspiratorial, drawing my own as though we shared a great secret. After what seemed like a long time, I felt it. A movement. A delicate tremor radiating from my Ma's deep body, as though my touch like a signal had drawn it outward to me.

The drawn shades darken the afternoon room. Ma, holding Joan, rocks slowly back and forth, humming softly. She cradles Joan in her left arm, positioning the small mouth onto the amber circle. Joan's small gripping hands dimple the flesh of Ma's breast. They seem folded absolutely into one another within the soft lateral tiers of blankets that interweave them.

Then, unexpectedly, Aunt Erica enters the room. For a moment she just stands in the doorway, hands on hips.

"Why, I'm downright surprised at you, Mary Jane," Aunt Erica says. "Letting the boy watch you doing that."

"For heaven's sake why? He's just a little boy."

"That is just the point. He hadn't ought to be seeing such things. For his own good he hadn't. It will set him to wondering about things."

Aunt Erica takes me from the room.

The photograph is of Catherine and Ma standing together on Aunt Erica's front steps. It is summertime and the dresses they wear are sleeveless. Both are smiling and because of the bright sunlight their eyes are squinted into narrow lines. Both look so much younger than my memories of them, and they appear to be very happy about something. Perhaps Ma is happy because she is pregnant, at least eight months pregnant judging from the picture. The contours of her swollen body are clearly visible through her thin cotton dress. She is pregnant with me.

As I look at Ma's swollen body I try to imagine myself floating somewhere inside of her. I try to imagine how my face looked then and how my body is shaped. And I wonder if I am awake or asleep in that instant the shutter clicks. I look at Ma's and Catherine's smiling faces and I think about that captured moment before I was born. I think about the fact that they do not know who I am. And there, only inches within my Ma's body, I am waiting to make them both real.

I had noticed how Mary would frequently place her hand, palm down, fingers spread wide, against her abdomen. Then, very quietly, she would poise with that stillness of expectant waiting. When I asked her why she did this, she told me that sometimes she thought she could actually feel it alive inside her body. That was impossible, I told her, because it was much too early for something like a movement.

I know that, she said. But it isn't a movement I feel. I mean, it's just the fact that something is growing in there. That it's alive and feeding from my body. More than that even, because it *is* a part of my body. I mean in a way it is. It's me and not me at the same time.

You're wrong about it being alive, I told her. It's just some wet dark hunk chowing down in your gut. It's not a person. Just a bloody hunk. You wouldn't recognize anything human about it. It would look like a fish or some shit.

Well, it's alive. What's inside my body is alive.

That's just some of your Catholic crap.

It's alive.

Under the circumstances, I'd avoid that sort of thinking if I were you.

You're not me though.

Four

Catherine.

Because she was often high as a kite, and also because she was often crazy as a loon, Catherine made for swell company. On Saturdays I usually went along with her to the library to read in the kids' room until she closed up at noon (thanks to Catherine's efforts the high school library served also as the community library and, besides Saturday mornings, she kept it open on her own time several evenings a week). After Catherine had closed up, we would usually mosey over to Murphy's five-and-dime store on Front Street, where we would browse casually about the counters of trinkets and toys. The five-and-dime was one of our favorite joints to hang out. It was especially neat on rainy or snowy days when everything seemed folded in on itself, like the air, with all of its old candy and fresh popcorn and people smells pressing gently against my face as I walked slowly along the narrow aisles. And there was always music coming from somewhere, usually hillbilly music, which spread softly throughout the whole store. I liked to watch the bored, powdered faces of the salesgirls, whose hair seemed always to be bleached blond and had colored ribbons perched in it like little birds. And they were always chewing gum, it seemed: their mouths moving in strange, steady rotations which made me think of fish eating.

Catherine and I always spent a lot of time in the pet department. She usually liked to watch the birds, mostly canaries and colorful parakeets, as they fluttered around to nowhere in their cramped cages. I usually liked to look at the turtles and the fish. The turtles were very small and they lived in strange little glass-sided swamps on the counters. There were so many of them that sometimes they had to live on top of one another. Many of them had painted shells. They cost a dime each. The fish, mostly angelfish and goldfish, darted like little pieces of light about the bright aquariums, whose sides' thick glass was like a lens which made everything inside seem slightly larger than it actually was and which rarefied the green of the flowing plants and the cool colors of the pebbles. Sometimes a fish would swim up close to one of the sides and hover there, pressing its face near the glass as though it wanted to get a real good look at me.

After a time, Catherine and I would go to the store's fountain to eat our favorite lunch: double cherry Cokes and strange hotdogs. "Strange hotdogs" because we had a game of trying to outdo each other in thinking up weird crap to have the waitress put on them. Instead of getting the usual mustard or ketchup, we would with great nonchalance request peanut butter or jelly or both. The grand winner of our game was determined by whose order seemed to most nauseate the waitress. Since we ate there most Saturdays and since there were few waitresses, they all knew us well, and it seemed like they had their own game going to see who would get to wait on us. Also, as a sort of initiation I guess, whenever there was a new girl on the shift the other waitresses made sure she got to wait on us. Catherine won most of our games. Since the whole thing was a sort of dare between us, we had to eat everything we ordered or lose face; therefore I usually did not get myself too far out on a limb. Catherine, though, would try anything, especially if she had been nipping a lot that morning from the big brown medicine bottle which she always carried around in one of her huge purses. Once she had even sent a new waitress running frantically from us, hands pressed over mouth, gagging. Catherine had ordered a hotdog covered with chocolate syrup and chopped cashews.

After we ate lunch, Catherine and I would often go to the afternoon picture shows at the Kayton Theatre where, because Saturday was Kids' Kapers Day, several cartoons, a serial, and sometimes as many as three movies would be shown. The Kayton Theatre was another one of our favorite joints. While Catherine was buying us popcorn and junk at the candy counter, I would look at the stills of the movies behind the glass doors of the displays around the small lobby. If the stills were of movies I had seen before or of the serial from last week, I found that I could from memory fill in the action, the motions, on either side of each picture: the immediate before and the immediate after. The pictures were not really still at all, but were fluid, were film in my mind.

Usually I didn't sit with Catherine inside the theater. I liked to sit in the very front row. This way the show would fill up everything that I could see, and this made me feel like I was inside of it, that I was actually happening along with it. Also, I just didn't want to sit with Catherine. I didn't want any other kids to think that I had to have a grownup to take me to the movies. Anyhow, Catherine had her own favorite place to sit, which was as close to the very center of the audience as she could get. She liked being in the middle of the audience when she watched picture shows, she declared.

Almost always there was a Johnny Mack Brown or a Bob Steele or a Tim Holt Western showing. The serial was often a Western also: for instance, the Durango Kid, which was one of my very favorites. The Durango Kid seemed to have his black costume and mask and his white horse hidden out in every single cave of the Old West, so that whenever it was necessary he could make a sudden change into his secret self. This amazed me. And it was the basis of one of my favorite fantasies. For years when I was a kid I had old Halloween masks stashed out all around the neighborhood so that with but a moment's notice, I could leap behind a hedge and change myself into another being. I was a man of a thousand masks, I snickered secretly to myself. I was, indeed, the foremost phantom of my neighborhood. Anyway, besides the Westerns, also showing on the special Saturday feature card was usually a Bowery Boys or a Bud Abbott and Lou Costello comedy and sometimes there was a spook show. When there was a spook show I would always sit back in the middle of the audience with Catherine. I didn't want to sit up too close, alone, to a spook show. I didn't want to feel like I was inside of a spook show at all.

But I was. I was.

On our way to the library on many of those Saturday mornings, we would stop on the footbridge across Wade Creek and spit at floating objects in the brown, turning water, and even at the ducks, any of the eleven whites or three mallards, if they happened to swim near. Only, we did not, of course, spit tobacco spit like Grandpaw did, but just regular spit. Through the separation in her front teeth Catherine could aim almost as well as Grandpaw. She would aim steadily, slowly, then spit in a high, clear, careful arc, and if the selected target was hit, Catherine would call out, "Hot damn," and clap her hands.

On many of these mornings the fog from the river and from the creeks was spread thickly throughout the bottoms. On one particular morning, we stepped out into a soundless, unreal world: one transfigured by fog in which we were blind. Our steps dissolved before us. We walked but seemed to be motionless. Trees like apparitions emerged suddenly, darkly, as if they instead of we moved. I held close to Catherine and when at last we reached the bridge we stopped as usual, although below us the water with its targets moved invisibly. Catherine had been unusually quiet since we left the house, and for a time we just stood there, silently. Her face, white, smiling, was tilted slightly upward as if she expected something to appear above us. Her eyes, large to begin with, seemed to swell further from the effort of her intense watching. Finally, she spoke, though quietly. She told me that long ago, long before even the earth strata had buckled Appalachia into mountains, the spot we now stood upon had been the bottom of an inland sea. A sea which had for millions of years submerged all of this part of the North American continent. A sea which had receded had reap-

peared, and, finally, 300 million years ago, had receded
again. But, she told me, it will come once more. In the end,
this land will become sea again, for the earth is straining
itself back to water. I can feel its coming, she said. There is
the echo of dead surf in this fog. And in this fog there is
strange traffic. The ghosts of half-evolved fish, of half-
formed creatures caught dry as the sea died from the rising
mountains.

Catherine, contd.

I did not understand exactly what Catherine meant when
she once said, while laughing that strange, shrill laugh of
hers, that she was an archetypal old maid, even to the extent
of being a high school librarian. The word "archetypal" was
for a time what threw me, until she explained it as a word
meaning something weakly akin to "typical." I knew then
that what she was saying about herself she knew was not
really the case at all, for although she was an old maid all
right, she was not your basic high school librarian. I had, on
more than one occasion, had my friends repeat to me comments heard from their parents about old Catherine. Repeat,
my ass! The creeps would taunt me with them. That she
ought to be gotten rid of at the high school was the main
thing I heard, and this because, according to comments, she
was a crazy old maid who not only drank to excess but also
went in for smut. When once I asked Catherine about this
she said yes, they had a point all right, and that of all the
smut she went in for, dirty graffiti was her favorite. That
word threw me for a time also.

I know that because of the reading material she kept
available for the students in the library, Catherine's position
at the high school was threatened on several occasions from
various groups in our town. I remember once when Ma asked
her why she even worked as a high school librarian in the
first place, what with her money and her fine education, and

here she was just growing slowly old in a small town. Catherine simply smiled. She did not answer Ma. I remember I thought then that Catherine smiled and looked as though she had something mysterious up her sleeve.

Massive chests of drawers lined one wall of Catherine's sitting room, with all of the drawers stuffed full of her many collections of small petrified fossils, and of natural casts, and of the prints of ferns in shale partings, and of the rare shells she had acquired during her travels. On many evenings I would go with her to her rooms, and together, alone, we would take the small, cool, fossiled rocks and the shells from the drawers. We would observe them closely: holding, feeling them, as though the quiet rub of stone or shell to flesh might in itself stir recognition. For, as Catherine said, the mystery of it all is held in stone and shell. One evening she gave me a special fossil for my own which held the tract of a small worm's burrowing that could possibly be, she told me, as old as a billion years.

Catherine traveled for at least two of the three months of every summer. When she returned she brought strange things back with her.

To bring strange things back is the true function of trips, she told me. There is a very basic instinct within each of us for familiarity. To properly follow this feeling one must make the strange and curious as commonplace as possible. How else can one negate the coldly inhuman indifference of things? How else?

When she was twenty-two, Catherine had finished the work for her master's degree in English literature at Marshall College in Huntington, West Virginia. (Since 1963, Marshall has been a university. In 1970, it made nationwide headlines when its whole football team was wiped out in a plane crash on a foggy mountain.) The following summer, Catherine had set out on the first of her travels, or "expeditions" as she called them. She toured leisurely through the deep South, lingering for any stay only in Miami and then again later in New Orleans. She found that the hot nights oppressed her and that she could not sleep. She spent them in cheaply rented hotel rooms (by choice), sitting naked before slow electric fans, sipping J. T. S. Brown whiskey over crushed ice, and writing in that collapsed, nearly illegible hand of hers on long, yellow-paged tablets. Writing a novel.

After five years of sending it off to big name publishing houses Catherine had finally published her novel herself, having two hundred copies printed up and clothbound by a firm in Columbus, Ohio. The binding was yellow, with severely plain black lettering, the letters all lower case. It was a beautiful job and cost a pile. Since she managed to sell only twenty-two copies of her book, very little of her investment was redeemed. Thirty-seven other copies she gave away to an exhaustive list of her immediate friends, her old friends, and even her more than casual acquaintances. After selecting one copy for her own shelves, one that she placed between copies of *As I Lay Dying* and *Miss Lonelyhearts*, she stored the remainder in a trunk in the attic. A gesture of safekeeping, she called it. For she did not want such obviously valuable property simply lying carelessly about where just anyone might get at it.

Because of her collector's instinct Catherine had saved the seventeen rejection slips that she had received over the five years. With great care she had backed them delicately upon black velvet, like pinned butterflies, and had framed them in a gold-gilded, rococo-rimmed frame which she then hung in her bathroom on the wall directly opposite the commode.

Her safekeeping gesture of storing the remaining books in the trunk in the attic failed, though, for they were mostly eaten, as she discovered several years later when, on an impulse, she looked into the trunk. Just by what devious means mice could have penetrated such an apparently secure trunk, Catherine claimed she could never really divine. She simply declared that they must have, as in the old wives' tale, literally generated themselves into hungry life from that cloudy, frostlike mold that she had found spreading in interlacing circular blossoms across what was left of the books' decaying cloth sides.

Catherine, contd.

Because, Catherine said, many people considered its unusual markings to symbolize the birth, crucifixion, and resurrection of Christ, the sand dollar is often called the Holy Ghost Shell. On the top side of the shell an outline of the Easter lily can be traced. Then, in the lily's center, there appears a five-pointed star which represents the Star of Bethlehem. Symbolic of the four nail holes and the spear wound made in Christ's body are the five narrow openings. Both the Christmas poinsettia and the bell can be recognized in outline on the shell's bottom. Then, when broken open, the shell reveals five small birds, which are called the Doves of Peace. Some say these doves represent the angels that sang the first Christmas morning to the shepherds.

This, Catherine told me, was an example of how things become real. Since they have no true value of their own, the things of the world must acquire it. And they acquire it from us. This is how they participate in our reality, one that ultimately transcends them. Indeed, one that ultimately transcends us. And it is all like this, she said. All colors, all textures, the shape of all things, even time and space: they are all illusionary movements of intuition.

Of all the family, Catherine wrote only to me during the time she was in the sanitarium. I felt important to receive the only letters from her: letters from a place almost the same as a crazy house, addressed directly to me: letters from a person whose whispered name was like a cold draft under the doors of our house. In one of her early letters to me she wrote that the sanitarium was too expensive, too plush of a place for her to pull off a proper pedagogical suicide, that an abject sacrifice needs an abject joint. Because of my feeling of self-importance and because the words "suicide" and "sacrifice" both intrigued and frightened me, I showed the letter to others of the family, and this was a stupid mistake. Of course, they had no ideas at all about what Catherine was getting at, and, also, some jive developed as to whether I should be permitted to receive such mail, even if it did come from Catherine. Stupid, fat Aunt Hilda said:

—Letters from a sick woman like her are bound to be downright unhealthy for a kid his age. And such talk about suicide and all is un-Christian.

—Let the boy alone, Uncle Charlie said. Let him keep his letters.

—Why don't you just keep your face shut! Hilda said.

—He can take the letters, Aunt Erica said.

Not to take any more chances, from that time on I tried to keep the letters strictly to myself. And not just because I was afraid the family might try to get their hands on them, but also because I had discovered a peculiar guilt in myself for having shown the letter around in the first place. I had begun to sense the quiet privacy of what old Catherine wrote to me; and although she would have never thought to burden a snot-nosed kid like myself with any pledge of any such privacy, I knew it somehow. I tried to keep the letters hidden, even developing a complex and satisfying ritual of frequently moving them from secret place to secret place. I have always suspected, however, that most if not all of the letters were eventually found and examined by others of the family, especially by Hilda. This irritated the hell out of me, for by then

I had begun also to sense that Catherine was not actually writing to me at all, at least not exactly to the nine-year-old me, but rather to some hidden witness she intuited waiting within me. And the very imagined picture of Hilda hovering over Catherine's letters in stupid, confused frustration, and from this frustration, calling her words crazy, angered me to the edges of hate. But hate has its good points, I found. For I can recall with pleasure the many, many happy hours I spent imagining gruesome tortures, delightfully slow deaths, for dear old Aunt Hilda.

As Moses lifted up the serpent in the wilderness, even so must the Son of man be lifted up.

Do not forget that the moon is the first of all creatures to die. But do not forget either that the moon is the first to live once again. And after three days without fail the maidens return among us from the forest huts.

Do not forget that God has three keys. There is the key of the rain. There is the key of the morning of birth. There is the key of the rising of the dead.

And Catherine wrote:

There was once a man who went to seek God in the solitude of an island in the heart of an inland sea. This man resigned himself to prayer with a vow that he would remain on the island, which was a harsh, forsaken place, until he spoke to God's revealed face. By day the hermit would sit in absolute silence beneath the shadows of the larger rocks. He would watch the moonlight's cool whiteness move through the night across the face of the still sea toward where he sat. He remained alone like this for a long time. Years went by as he waited. It happened finally that on one hot midafternoon the hermit observed a movement on the distant water. Because the sun's glare was very hard he was not certain at first of what he saw. It seemed to move from the far horizon slowly across the water toward his island. Presently, he saw that it was a ship. Because he had been alone for so very long and because of his good nature the hermit welcomed the visitors, who were fishermen stopping for rest and fresh water.

Now there was among these men one who was obviously afflicted in his mind. Flies walked unnoticed by him upon his face and into his sagging mouth. He was just a poor fool the men said, who they permitted to do menial tasks for his sustenance. Upon further questioning the hermit found that the man had never been christened, for, as the men said, what was the use as he could not understand anyway. And, of course, he knew no prayers. While the fishermen rested the hermit began to speak to the fool of God and to teach him a simple prayer. By the time the men got up that evening to leave, the hermit had succeeded in teaching the fool the simple prayer. The men were pleased by this; it was a good omen. The fool seemed very happy that he could please his friends.

When the men had left his island the hermit withdrew again into his solitude and silence, and he sat upon the beach waiting quietly for the moonlight. He sat for what seemed a long time deep in his own thoughts and in his special longing to know God. The moonlight at last lit the sea and moved as always across the waters toward where he sat in darkness. But on this night he saw also something else out there. A figure ghostly paled by the moon was walking the waters toward the island. The figure approached slowly. In amazement the hermit waited quietly. At last the figure came up on the sand of the moonlit beach and walked slowly to where the hermit sat.

—I forgot the prayer, the fool said, the lips of his sagging mouth shining with drool.

—So who needs it, the hermit told him.

I used to have the only remaining copy of Catherine's novel that I knew about. I managed to save it from the piles of her personal belongings that members of the family helped to sort from her rooms. They had to spend a full morning carting all of her collections away. Most of the glass pieces and the artifacts Hilda kept, getting her fat paws on them right off the bat. The shells and rocks and fossils Aunt Erica eventually sold or threw away. The ritual masks and the beads were stored in the attic. Later, Aunt Erica destroyed them. They were un-Christian things to have, she said. Dear old Ma took the prints and the woodcuts. In a like manner all the rest of the collections were dispersed. I got hold of the book. It has since disappeared. I have no damn idea what happened to it. I remember how weird it was though: about a strange haunted woman who spent many hours each night walking through the dark rooms of a decaying mansion in search of a never named object. And I remember that Catherine had included a page index of her "signs, symbols, and sundry archetypes," and that she had dedicated it to all "assistant professors on the make." Old Catherine was a real caution.

Late July 1949.

On Sunday mornings Catherine was of the habit of strolling leisurely into town to buy her newspapers. Although she never attended any services, she would often wait for Cynthia and me after church so that we could all walk home together.

Cynthia ran down the alley ahead of me toward where Catherine was waiting. Her thin legs were quick and as she ran her feet churned a spray of small gravel and dust up into the air behind her. I could not run fast enough to close in on her and so she reached Catherine a good distance ahead of me. By the time I reached them my side was hurting. Cynthia was not even breathing hard.

"Well, I was beginning to think you two were not going to show up," Catherine said, a cigarette dangling absently

from her mouth. She was sitting on top of one of the four
bright, apparently new, garbage cans that were lined along
the hedges of the parsonage fence. Her hair was twined
tightly up around several large yellow rollers. A half-dozen
thick Sunday papers were piled on her lap.

"We had to cut down through the kindergarten and the
kitchen to shake off Hercules," Cynthia told her.

"Yeah, and Cynthia creamed him," I said.

"Indeed?" Catherine said.

"I did not cream him!"

"You did so. I was right there and saw it."

"Did you really strike your poor little hapless cousin?"
Catherine asked. She had hopped down from the can and was
adjusting the papers under each arm.

"Well, yes, I hit him. But I did not cream him. Just a
little old tap is all. The fat slob was tagging along and I
didn't want his big mouth yakking around today."

"Well, let us all settle down," Catherine said. "And get a
move on. All we need is to be late for dinner and get everyone in an uproar. My feeble head is not up to any uproar
today."

"Are you going to let me puff on your cigarette?" Cynthia
asked.

"Perhaps."

"Please. Please."

"I said perhaps."

Cynthia ran ahead of Catherine and me, returning only
to report things of possible interest which waited ahead. One
time, as Catherine and I rounded a hedged corner, we saw
Cynthia a little distance ahead doing what appeared to be a
dance by the side of the road. When we approached her we
saw that she was doing a graceful tiptoe about the scattered
blackish balls of horse shit.

By the time we reached Parker Street in the lower west
end of town my heavy leather shoes felt like stones tied to
my feet. The thick cordlike strings had already come loose

three times. The last time I had had to stop to retie them, I
had bunched them into intricate knots.

Parker Street was a vague two blocks long. It had once
been paved at its east end with bricks, but the black macadam patches were now so frequent that only a few uncovered spaces of the old brick remained. The houses at this
paved end of the road had once been the homes of minor
coal company officials. Now they were the homes of the more
well-off of Century's negro population. The paved-patched
road disappeared at the beginning of Parker's second, rather
ill-defined block. There was no gradual sinking away. The
road seemed to be simply swallowed by the packed hardened
clay. Here was where one end of the Old Clay Road began.
The small frame houses that were clustered on both sides
of this end of the road had once been coal company houses
also, but ones for the miners themselves. Now, only negroes
lived in the ones that were not boarded up.

When Catherine and I reached where the clay road began
we found Cynthia waiting for us. She was in the front yard
of one of the boarded-up houses, sitting straddled upon an
old rusted-out car hood which looked like the shell of some
giant tortoise resting there in the weeds.

"What took youall so long?" she asked.

"Old age and sinful habits, my dear," Catherine said.

Small beads of perspiration were lined along Catherine's
forehead and upper lip, and dark stains spread like webs
through the cotton of her blouse under her arms. Cynthia
jumped up from the hood and began to brush the rusty
smears from the back of her dress and legs. The smears
looked like faint hazes of dried blood.

"I ran into some nosy niggers up the road," Cynthia said,
as she came into the road toward us.

"Now, now, young lady," Catherine said. "We have no
need to talk like that."

"Well, what else can you call them? That's just what they

are. They just stand there staring at you like they can't get
their eyes full."

"Where are they?" I asked.

"Up at that shack at the turn of the road. A whole stinky
tribe of them."

"Well, dear, we will just ignore them," Catherine said.
"There is no need to let the butt-hole behavior of others dis-
turb us."

When we started to walk on, Cynthia held back with
Catherine and me. As we approached the road's bend, Cynthia gestured toward a small frame house on our left. Several
adult negroes were sitting or standing about its sagging front
porch. More than a dozen kids were playing in the dirt yard
around the house, some climbing about an old wheel-less car
which rested, rusting slowly away, upon cinderblocks. Two
little girls, apparently playing dress-up, were draped in
brightly flowered plastic sections of a torn curtain. One boy
had the wire frame of a lampshade over his head. It looked
like a strange cage.

As soon as we had come into view all of their eyes riveted
upon Cynthia. The adults quit their talking and the children
their play, and they all simply stared at us, at Cynthia, as we
passed.

"I told youall they were a bunch of nosy niggers," Cynthia
said.

"Hush," Catherine said.

"Well they are."

"Hush."

When we reached the far end of the yard, Cynthia turned
suddenly and yelled:

"Fuck you, nosy niggers!"

For a time as we walked on down the Old Clay Road, Catherine did not say anything. Nobody said anything. Trees grew

in dense clusters on either side of the narrow road. Their branches were thick and low and they arched across the road, meeting and interweaving. A heavy gloom, like blue still smoke, was settled underneath. Often we had to step around rain pools, whose dark surfaces were hazed with the wisping blues and golds of slime. We walked and walked. Finally Catherine told Cynthia that she understood how she felt. She was still, however, disappointed in the way Cynthia behaved. But let's just forget the whole thing, Catherine said. Cynthia did not say anything in reply. We walked along again without talking. It was not fun as it usually was when we all walked home together. Where the road began to bend toward the river, the woods opened into a small cleared area. This was where we saw the man. He was lying beside the road.

Catherine quickly walked over to where he was lying in a slight depression at the road's edge. Cynthia followed right behind her. I followed them up.

"Who is it?" Cynthia asked.

"I'm not certain," Catherine said, as she bent over him peering intently into his face. "I do believe, though, that he is poor old Boomer Bill."

"Ugh, that pig," Cynthia said.

"Is he dead or something?" I asked.

"Dead drunk," Catherine said.

Boomer Bill was lying on his side, his knees drawn up toward his chest, his arms wrapped about his head. His clothes were old and torn and on his face was several days' growth of beard. From his open mouth a brown tube of hardened vomit spread in a semicircle onto the ground in front of his face. Flies buzzed all about him, walking on his face, on the dried vomit, walking in and out of his mouth.

"Ugh," Cynthia said. "He stinks. What a piggy bum."

"How observant," Catherine said.

"Let's get out of here," I said.

"Ugh, yes," Cynthia said.

"Well, let's see if we can do something for him first," Catherine said.

She stood for another moment just looking down at Boomer, then she walked past him off the road into the shade of a nearby tree. She began to spread out her Sunday papers, unfolding them in sections and shaping them into a wide rectangle on the ground. Then, with great difficulty, and crinkling her nose at the smell, she began trying to maneuver Boomer onto the papers. Cynthia and I just watched.

"How can you even touch him?" Cynthia asked.

Boomer moaned several times, and once waved his hand feebly in front of his face, as Catherine pulled and pushed him. Finally she had tugged him onto the papers. She stood erect then and rolled her fists along the small of her back.

"This old doll has just completed her physical exertion quota for a solid month," Catherine said. "Two months!"

She spread several other papers out over Boomer's face.

"That might help to keep a few flies off," she said. "When we get home I'll call the sheriff for someone to come take care of him."

"Why are you helping this smelly old bum?" Cynthia asked. "Aunt Erica says that they are the scum of the earth."

"Empathy," Catherine said.

"What does that mean?"

"Recognition, my dear."

Five

Early September 1949.

Small spider webs sparkle in the damp grass. The morning air is warm, and although I have to wear a sweater, I can play outdoors. I have a shoebox full of little metal men whom I use for my battles. Some of them are soldiers, others are cowboys and Indians. In the side yard there is a small brick-circled flower garden. Once a man used to grow roses there. He was Aunt Erica's brother who lived in this house for a long time and he used to win prizes with his roses. But he died. Only dry stalks are there now, and layers of old leaves, because no one even rakes it anymore. I use it for my battles.

To start my battle I put the soldiers and the cowboys along one edge of the garden and then I set up the Indians on the other side. Sometimes, I make the battles go on all through the morning, until nearly all of the men are killed off. I always make the Indians lose in the end. They are supposed to lose because they are way outnumbered and because in real life they lost. Except for that one battle Catherine once told me about, when General Custer and his soldiers were all killed off. But I never make that battle. I just don't see how the soldiers and cowboys could ever lose, and so since I can't understand it I never make that battle.

One particular metal soldier is my favorite. Unlike most of the others he still has much of his original color, and even his small painted face has not been chipped away. I always make him the captain of the other men and I make him do brave things, such as leading the charges or crawling out onto the battlefield under fire to help his wounded soldiers. Sometimes, I pretend this soldier is myself, and that he does what I would do. Other times I pretend that he is my dear old Pop. In either case he is the bravest of all the men in battle.

When he is me, I pretend that although he is often seriously shot up he never stops fighting, and I never let him die. Sometimes, however, when he is my dear old Pop I let him die from his wounds. When I do this I always throw a big funeral for him, sometimes spending as much time on it as I spend on the battle itself. I always dig his small grave in the very center of the flower bed and sometimes I leave him buried there for several hours, once even for overnight. This makes it seem like he was really killed off and that it is not just all pretend. I can make his funeral seem sadder this way. Then, later, when I dig him up again and set him out in front of his army to fight some more, I feel like a million bucks.

The warm morning in early September. I have my men all fixed around where I want them and the battle is half-finished. But then Hercules comes along and for no reason at all begins knocking my men down. He kicks them around and scatters them out in the grass. Some he picks up and throws as far away as he can. I run at him but he catches my arms and then he trips me. Once he gets me down he sits on my stomach. He begins pulling up handfuls of grass and rubbing them slowly over my face. If I eat three handfuls he'll let me up, he says. I tell him that I'll tell Aunt Erica if he doesn't let me up. He tells me that I still have a lesson or two to learn and that he's going to be my teacher. He pulls up more grass and keeps rubbing it in my face and pushing it into my mouth.

When the rock hits his head Hercules screams and rolls off me onto the ground. Quick as a flash he is up again and running toward Cynthia. When he gets the second rock on his head he falls down again. His head is bleeding in two places and he rolls around on the grass crying and holding the cuts as though he is trying to push the blood back in. Cynthia runs over and jumps on his back, then holds his arms down. She tells me to come on over and do anything I want to him to get even. I kick his side three times. Cynthia asks is that all I want to do to him? So I kick him three more times. When Cynthia lets him up he runs toward Aunt Erica's house screaming. Blood is all over the grass.

Cynthia finds the two rocks she threw. She rubs them in the grass then puts them in her jeans' front pockets. They are smooth and round and are her favorite throwing stones. She is a deadeye with those stones. So then we start looking around through the grass for my men, but we can't find all of them. There are four missing. One cowboy, two Indians, and, worst of all, my favorite soldier, the captain. Cynthia tells me not to worry because she will help me look around for it all day if necessary. We'll find that soldier no matter what, she says. So we look and look.

Then we see Aunt Hilda. She is coming across the yard toward us faster than I have ever seen her move before. When she gets near us, Cynthia jumps out of her reach.

"You come here right now!" Aunt Hilda yells. "And by God I mean right this minute!"

"You must think I'm stupid or something," Cynthia calls back to her. "If you want to get your fat hands on me you'll have to catch me."

Aunt Hilda starts toward Cynthia, chasing after her around the yard. Sometimes Cynthia lets Aunt Hilda get very near and then jumps away in the last second, running and laughing. Aunt Hilda's face is red and she is puffing for air. Aunt Hilda is fat as a cow. Soon, she stops running and just stands there panting for breath.

"This time you've gone too far, girlie!" Aunt Hilda barks between pants. "I don't care what anyone says, this time you're gonna get it good!"

"You have to catch me first, Auntie Poo," Cynthia says and begins to dance in circles around where Hilda is standing, staying just out of her reach. Cynthia begins to sing:

Hilda Hilda two by four
can't get through the bathroom door
so she does it on the floor

Aunt Hilda grabs me. I did not even get a chance to duck. I was watching Cynthia and laughing.

"Now, you little devil, you get over here fast or he gets what's in store for you!"

"I guess you better come on over now," I tell Cynthia.

"You get your dumb fat paws off him!" Cynthia yells. "He didn't hit your stupid kid!"

"Are you coming or does your little brother get it for you?"

"You let him go! You better let him go!"

Hilda jerks me up by my arm and slaps my head.

"Well, are you coming to take your medicine or not?"

"Hey, Cynthia, please come on," I call to her.

Hilda begins to slap around my head again. She slaps me over and over. My ears start to buzz.

When the rock thuds into her shoulder, Hilda lets loose of my arm. I fall to the ground and quickly roll out of her reach. She just stands there staring at Cynthia and holding the place on her shoulder where the rock struck. Her mouth is wide open and her eyes look half popped out of her head.

Cynthia stands in front of Hilda with her arm drawn back ready to throw another stone.

"I'll clobber you with the other one," Cynthia says. "And this time I'll throw it hard as I can if you don't get out of here and leave us alone."

After another moment Hilda turns away from us without saying a single word and begins waddling quickly back toward the house.

I pick up Cynthia's throwing stone from the grass and take it over to her.

"Well, that's that," she says.

"I bet you get whipped or something," I tell her.

"Nobody will lay a single finger on me."

"But I bet you get punished somehow. I bet they won't let you listen to the radio for a long time."

"Big deal. I'll just sneak in and listen to it with Kitty."

"Will you still help me look some more for that lost soldier? He has to be around here somewhere."

"Sure. Why not."

So we go back to looking around. We look and look. But we never find the lost soldier.

Caller.

Vincent Dipero was a hot shit hero. He had been the first soldier not only from Century but from the whole southern section of the county to be wounded in the European theater during World War II. Indeed, he had been one of the earliest casualties in the entire state. Vincent Dipero was a hero all right. He had left the flesh, the bone, and the blood of his wholeness over in a foreign land for his country's sake. Vince had lost his left leg.

Speer Whitfield, that kid within whom I more or less successfully lurked, was too young to be at the train depot with the rest of the town to meet Vince and his artificial leg's homecoming. This was too bad, because Speer would have surely enjoyed the festivities. A lot of local men were dressed up in their various uniforms, including a few members of the county's K.K.K. Two bands were there to play. Even the state attorney general was on hand. A grand time was had by all.

A year after his triumphant return, Vince was elected the sheriff of Kanawha County for the first of his four terms in that office. And it was as a sheriff called upon because of trouble that he first came into Speer Whitfield's life.

October 1949.

It was trouble that Cynthia later said she had known was headlong on its way the moment she was first awakened by the sounds of the heavy boots stomping up the street through the early morning stillness. As though drawn by a weird magnet, the man had turned in at Aunt Erica's front gate and had headed up through the yard toward the porch. He probably had seen the swing from the road and had decided that it was time for a little snooze, for the swing was what he headed directly toward, clomping across the porch boards and stretching out on it with one dangling leg pushing up and back:

eeeeeeeeeeeeeeeeeeeeeeeeeeeeeeeeeeaaaaaaaaaaakkkkkkk
aaaaaaaaaaaaaaaaaaeeeeeeeeeeeeeekkkkkkkkkkkk

"Wake up, Speer! Wake up!" Cynthia had shaken me and was across the room at the window by the time I managed to stir fully awake. She was peeking toward the porch from behind the slightly pulled curtains. *Come here,* she signaled to me. *Out there,* she pointed to the porch. Like a huge eye the glowing circle looked in from the night. Cynthia caught my arm as I swirled to run like hell.

"It's only an ol' drunk miner," she whispered and giggled. "He's lying out there swinging as drunk as a skunk. His helmet light is turned on."

Then, suddenly, Ma was there in the dark room with us. "What is it out there?" she whispered.

I could smell her face cream and powder as she came near.

"A drunk man," Cynthia said and giggled again. She was jumping up and down excitedly, her white cotton nightgown seeming to make her movements glow in the darkness.

Then, suddenly, Aunt Erica was with us also.

"What's all the uproar out there?" she asked, her voice angry.

Ma motioned frantically at her to hush down.

"A drunk on the porch," Cynthia told again.

"God only knows what he's up to," Ma whispered. "Probably some nigger out to rape and pillage."

"Just shut that foolishness up right now," Aunt Erica said. "Now you get in there on the phone to Charlie, Mary Jane!"

"You know he's not home tonight," Ma said.

"Don't you remember, Aunt Erica," Cynthia said, "he's on business down in Hinton tonight?"

"Well, Mary Jane, get in there calling the sheriff. Now get going!" Aunt Erica said. "And try to wake Kitty up while you're at it."

Aunt Erica turned to Cynthia and me. She told us to stay put over in bed, and that she meant just that! to stay put in this room, in this bed even if the house caught on fire and burned to the ground! She turned quickly from us toward the hall door and was gone. Then, only moments later, suddenly, the porch light exploded brightness across the front of the house and the yard and the front door's double-glass panel shook near to shattering in a slam. And from the very heart of all that bright noise, we heard:

"You had best get a move on!" Aunt Erica's angry voice.

Cynthia flashed to the window again. I followed her.

The dark, oiled barrels of the shotgun gathered light into rich orange beads along its clean lines. Aunt Erica shuddered her thin back into an arch to balance the heavy swing up to sight and she stood sideways toward the man with her elbow steadied high on her stuck-up hip.

"I said that you had best get a move on," she repeated.

The lower darkness of the man's face spread open smiling to show an even assortment of white and gold teeth. The black encircling grime of his face made his inner mouth seem deep red and very moist.

"I'll tell you just once more!" Aunt Erica said.

The heaviness of the gun's barrels was making her arms

tremble and her rimless glasses were fogging over. The man held out toward her his quarter-full, label-less bottle, its liquid flushing yellowish in the porch light. He asked would she like a little drink or a little kiss first. He then rolled his wet red inner lips over for Aunt Erica's approval and gave for good measure a long sight of his bright tongue.

"I'll blast your drunk fool head off is what I'll do!" Aunt Erica said, her voice tight with anger, and the trembling of her arms stopped. "I can't tell clearly if you're white or colored under all that coal dust but you mind that I'd make a white widow quick as a nigger. I'm not prejudiced. I'll shoot any color of man!"

"C'mon ol' bat, a li'l kis a li'l drinkie."

"You stay put, mister. I've called the law and the sheriff is on his way this very minute."

Cynthia had gone into the hall and she started to click the porch light on and off quickly.

"You just stop that foolishness right now, Cynthia Whitfield!" Aunt Erica yelled, never removing her eyes from the man.

How did she know that it was Cynthia doing it, I wondered.

The man began laughing uproariously. He waved his bottle at the flashing light. Then he started to push himself up awkwardly from the swing.

The shot's blast seemed to hang in the shattered air forever. And it joined coiling into Ma's scream. The miner was rolled tightly into a quivering ball on the damp, slick-looking boards. He was moaning. I could hear Cynthia clapping and laughing from the hallway. Ma stood pressed back to the bedroom's far wall like a frozen flower of its paper.

Then I heard the siren.

As Vince Dipero came quickly up the yard through the

leaves toward the porch, I noticed that he ran with a limp.
I noticed also that Vince was several steps ahead of his
deputy.

"Did you shoot him, Miss Whitfield?" Vince asked when
he reached the porch.

"Not yet," Aunt Erica said. "I just shot out in the yard to
cool him off a mite. But I have me another loaded barrel if
I find I need it."

"Well, ma'am, I'd say offhand you done cooled this bird
right off," Vince said, laughing.

"You ain't gonna find a man cooler," the deputy said.

"I been shot," the man said from under the crouch of his
arms.

"C'mon, buddy," Vince said as he pulled the miner to his
feet.

"I'm bleeding," the man said.

"Let's get a look at you, buddy," Vince said. "Well, you
again is it, Collier. I'll be damn."

The bottle had smashed under the miner when he fell to
the porch, and he gripped the dark wet stains and told Vince
to look at all the blood. He had been shot and was bleeding
to death, he told Vince. Then he pointed toward Aunt Erica,
telling Vince that that old bat standing over there was crazy
as hell and dangerous to boot. The deputy picked the
miner's helmet up from the porch and replaced it awkwardly
on his head. Its lamp still burned but was lost in the porch
light's brightness.

"That ain't the way to talk to a lady, Collier," Vince said,
then said to Aunt Erica that he'd just get this bird off to the
clink right now.

Aunt Erica asked Vince why he couldn't just park the
miner out in the county car for a few minutes so that he and
his deputy could come on in for some hot coffee, seeing how
it was near morning and how they had come on out to help
her and all. A good hot cup of coffee would sure stay that first-

light chill, she told Vince. And besides, she said, there were some pretty well scared people indoors. Vince's presence would surely help calm them down.

Vince said that he would do just that. That he would take her right up on that coffee, but said that his deputy would have to take a raincheck as he had best get their mutual friend Collier on off to the clink.

"You get directly on back here after me now," Vince told his deputy, then said to Aunt Erica why didn't she just go on in and he'd be right along as soon as he helped his deputy get their friend out to the car.

"Well, I'll go get the water started," Aunt Erica said.

As she reached the front door she stopped and shook her finger at the miner. She told him that he had best get himself straightened up before it was too late, that he had best get right down on his knees and pray for help.

When Aunt Erica entered the door, Vince stood for a few moments quietly watching the front of the house. Then, after spitting out into the yard, he turned and walked slowly over to the miner and deputy. The miner was shaking his head as though it was still ringing from the blast. He still gripped the wet front of his shirt. I stayed by the front window. I could hear Aunt Erica and Ma and Cynthia talking in back toward the kitchen and then I heard running water.

Vince had flexed his fist deep into the miner's stomach and pulled it back before I even registered the motion. Then, more deliberately, as the miner hunched over vomiting, Vince chopped quickly at the side of his neck. As the miner sagged forward, his helmet falling off and smashing its lamp on the porch boards, Vince caught him. He hoisted the man up again, standing him back flat on his feet. From the side the deputy helped brace the man steady. Vince stood back just looking at the miner, his left thumb hooked over his gunbelt buckle, and said so quietly that I could scarcely hear him through the glass:

"Well, we told you, buddy. We told you plain as the nose on your ugly face what would happen if we caught you out raising hell again."

Vince swung, hitting smack in the center of the miner's face. The miner fell backward, arms loose and flapping like crazy wings, off the porch into the yard. Leaves fluttered up about where he thudded onto the ground. They drifted down onto his chest and face.

After that, Vince started to come around, and not as a sheriff called on account of trouble. Vince was a caller of another sort. The son-of-a-bitch.

Six

On Decoration Day of the spring of 1950, Aunt Erica took the last of the seventeen tombstones, a gray marble one for her brother James' grave, to the family cemetery at the Old Homestead down in Logan County (that ancient, rambling, frame, log, and fieldstone house which had been constructed by my great- and great-great-grandfathers upon the very site and foundation of the original cabin that the first Whitfields in this part of the country had built back in the early 1800s), and she had had Uncle Charlie set it out with all the others on the slope above the house in the warm May afternoon sun.

Aunt Erica had spent forty-five years acquiring all the stones and now at long last she was finished. Her part of the collection was absolutely through, she had stated in no uncertain terms on that rainy April afternoon when she returned from selecting James' stone at Mr. Ketchum's monument lot, the fourth lot she had priced that month before feeling satisfied; but satisfied she was with Mr. Ketchum, the youngest mortician in town and a comer, everyone said, for he had but recently expanded his professional services successfully to include the monument trade, services to supplement those already included in his project south of town where he had begun to incorporate several rolling slopes of an old farm into burial lots whose reasonable rates marked them as good investments. Mr. Ketchum was a comer all right. He was quickly getting together a real corner in the burying business in our town.

Aunt Erica had come around the house and in the back way through the glassed-in back porch when she returned home from Mr. Ketchum's lot. I had been killing time standing at the front window in the dining room, just looking absently out into the hazed rainy air, which was almost a mist, and which caused my reflection in the glass to ghost spookily back at me (boo). As Aunt Erica had come around the wet brick walk, I ran from room to room along the side of the house, window to window, pulling aside the curtains and making faces at her. The bricks were very slick and Aunt Erica walked slowly, carefully watching her step, just as she always watched her step, and she did not see me until I knocked on the glass in the back bedroom; then she looked up, squinting her eyes in my direction. When she finally focused on me, she smiled and gave me a little wave. I stuck my tongue out at her then ran on back to the kitchen, announcing her homecoming to Catherine, who, for a remarkable change, was actually getting dinner that evening. Then I plopped down on the floor to play with my shoebox of seashells. Aunt Erica came directly into the kitchen and immediately sat down as though exhausted in the rocking chair beside the old coal stove, not even bothering to take off her raincoat which dripped into small, beading puddles on the bright waxed linoleum.

"Well, that's that," Aunt Erica said to Catherine, sighing. "Now it's all up to someone else in this family."

"Indeed?" Catherine said as she stirred something in a big pan on the gas stove.

"Well, I have provided for all the Whitfields who went before me. And now someone else will have to take care of all those who come after. Including me before too long, I reckon."

"Well, I am afraid it won't be me," Catherine said. "Besides, dear Auntie, you will outlive us all. You will be buying stones for us, every one."

"I didn't expect as much from you, anyway," Aunt Erica said.

"Well, I didn't expect you did. Besides, in my humble opinion, all you've done anyway is clutter up the fields again. Stuffing them all full of stones. And after generations of Whitfields worked years upon years clearing those rock and granite outcroppings. A waste of good space is what a graveyard is. 'Let the whiteness of bones atone to forgetfulness/ there is no life in them,' saith a poet. Anyway, I personally will not ever waste good space."

"Good lands to gracious," Aunt Erica said. "All you do is talk foolish."

"Alas! Indeed I do. Thank heavens! It is my truest asset. At any rate, I personally wish to approach eternity as ashes in an urn. As a still unravished bride of quietness. Alas, the foster child of silence and slow time. Oh, slow, slow time. Anyway, the only space I'll waste will be a few mere puny square inches on someone's bedroom mantel. No more space than a good old bottle of J. T. S. Brown would occupy. A mere few inches, 'tis all."

"If you'd give half a thought before you ran at the mouth, you'd make a lot more sense. And sense, heavens knows, is what you need. Or at least ought to make an appearance of. And by the way, that fine Mr. Ketchum surely gave me a good price on James' stone. You ought to pay him some mind, Kitty. He goes to our church, you know. And I understand he's been a widower five years now."

"Alas, indeed! Well, I guess I should. Especially if I'm planning to depart before too long. Indeed, I heard that he laid his first wife out himself. He even did up her hair himself. How touching."

"Well, now, there's not a thing in the world awrong with that. And, anyway, I wouldn't go believing just every blessed thing I happened to hear if I were you. All I know is that he gave me such a fine price on that stone and seemed a fine gentleman. He waited on me hisself, as he just happened to be at the lot, and he talked so nice and all. Just a fine person I'd say. He's got such pretty white dentures, too."

"Well, that truly now is a mark of quality," Catherine said. "But I would wager that his hands stink. I bet they smell just like formaldehyde."

"That is downright foolishness! Why, the Doctor used to have his hands in that stuff all the livelong time. And his hands never smelled in any such way. All I am saying is that you ought to pay him some mind. A dandy man like him. That is all I am saying."

"Ought I? Well, I suppose a thirty-seven-year-old dusty, spindly, eczema-ridden librarian does not exactly have a poke of opportunity does she? But by stars, I have a boyfriend, don't I, Speermint? You love your ugly old cousin in spite of everything, don't you?"

"Sure, I do, Kitty," I told her, and she bent down to fluff up my hair with her hand. I held the large pink fluted shell to my ear to hear the sea, but the refrigerator clicked on suddenly, humming the sound away. It was a magic sound, Catherine had always told me. A sound like no other that sung at once of where everything had been, had begun, and will be again at last.

Ma came into the kitchen from the front of the house, carrying a magazine and an empty glass.

"What's for chow tonight?" she asked Catherine.

"A virtual feast," Catherine said. "A sort of pseudo jambalaya, I think. But maybe not. I'll tell you more about it after I get up the nerve to taste it."

"Oh, crap!" Ma said. "Vince is coming around for dinner tonight. I might've known you'd pick tonight to get one of your cooking wild hairs."

"Well, no one told me anything about it, I'm afraid," Catherine said. "If I'd been aware Mr. Dipero was going to grace us with his presence I would have fixed up something more suitable to his gourmet sensibilities. Like some boiled catfish eyeballs garnished with a pinch of gorilla dandruff. Or, maybe, a good old-fashioned broiled goat's anus."

"You're just a downright riot," Ma said, drawing deeply on a cigarette which she had just lit, and then blowing small, perfect smoke rings in Catherine's direction.

"Yes," Aunt Erica said. "That Mr. Ketchum surely did do right by me on James' stone. Lands to gracious, I only wish I could have bought from him years ago."

Stones.

I can remember Aunt Erica telling about the stones and about the Doctor many times.

The first stone, she told, was a blue granite for her mother's grave that she had purchased in 1910. The next stone, purchased two years later, was for her father. The next was a big double stone for her grandparents. And so on, over the years. All of the first thirteen stones had been purchased jointly with her eldest brother, Dr. Alfonso Whitfield, who had actually thought of buying the stones for all the family in the first place.

He had talked about it the first time, Aunt Erica told (declaring that she could remember it like yesterday), once when they were just children on an early November morning, as they had come crunching through the frosted stubbly grass down the hill from the barn from milking, carrying pails of warm steaming milk, and had stopped at the small graveyard. It was enclosed by cow-wire in the lower east edge of what was then the high pasture and had at that time only five graves, she told. Alfonso's and her grandparents were buried there, and their Aunt Sarah, and first cousin Bob Hayhurst, and their younger brother James. James' grave was still covered with pine branches and cones to hide the dark, freshly turned earth. Small metal signs marked the graves and the older ones were already rust streaked. In the dim light none of the signs could be read from the fence. Alfonso and Erica had stood silently at the gate, stepping from foot to foot in the cold air, and watched the morning light begin to clear and glisten on the bleached grass and on the stripped, slick-looking trees.

—Someday I'm going to get big shiny headstones for every single one of them, Alfonso had said quietly. —And they'll be astanding for a hundred years. For a thousand. And folks can come around to see them and read and say, why, there's where James Whitfield or so-and-so got buried. And so no one will ever forget any Whitfields then. Not ever.

And he never forgot, Aunt Erica said.

When he grew to a man, he mined for a while, and then farmed, Aunt Erica told, and he even cruised timber on Piney River in Raleigh County. Then, one winter when he was working on a B & O Railroad grappling gang, clearing timber ahead of the track layers up the Holly River Valley, he boarded in the home of old Dr. Fullner. Come spring, Aunt Erica said, Alfonso seemed to know his direction in life. He went to Warnertown to the Center College, then two years later went to the Piedmont Medical College in Ohio. Three years later, in 1899, he came riding an old yellow claybank mare into the small logging camp at Turtle Bottom and set up his practice. Within two months, Aunt Erica told, he had operated successfully upon the first case of appendicitis ever diagnosed in the whole region. Seven years after the Doctor's first arrival, Aunt Erica came. Turtle Bottom was by that time the coal mining boom town of Hundred Mines, and was incorporated with its first mayor, Dr. Alfonso Whitfield, who was to go on in politics, she told, to be a six-term state senator, and also even a one-time Populist Party candidate, although unsuccessful, for a seat in Congress.

The Doctor had found his increasing responsibilities becoming quite a burden, and so he had sent for Aunt Erica to come and help him out, requesting also that she train to be his nurse. Aunt Erica had spent the two years since leaving the Gap Mills Women's College teaching in Summers County, where she had twelve full grades in the single room of an old log house whose ancient roof leaked just less rain than the puncheon floorboards could drain or absorb. She was only twenty then, Aunt Erica told, but, upon the Doctor's summons, she had spent half a month's salary on a brown-fleck walking mule and, alone, had ridge-traveled for two days to Hinton, then went by train to Beckley, where the Doctor met her, and they returned to Hundred Mines together.

And together, as neither ever married, they had bought the first thirteen stones, one by one, over many years, until

December 7, 1941, when the Doctor dispatched his brains with a shotgun, passing then forever into the frozen constellations of lore. Aunt Erica had had a small, pink marble mausoleum constructed for the Doctor, up under a high white sycamore on the south slope of the hill above the Homestead House, and she had collected the final four stones alone. But now she was finished. Now it was up to someone else in the family, she told the family.

The April and early May rains had flooded streams from the old drift mine shafts high on the ridges, and they poured down the steep watercourses and across the narrow dirt road that led up the hill to the Homestead House, washing the road out in several places into the lower hollows. Uncle Charlie had worried all month.

"Just not sure we'll be able to get that heavy stone up the hill," he had told Aunt Erica. "What with the road so bad."

"We'll get it up there if we have to carry it," she had told him. "I'll tote it up there myself, if need be. I'll be done with those things this Decoration Day and that's that. It's been forty years. I'll be through and that is that."

"Well, if the truck can't make it up, it can't make it."

"It had best."

Decoration Day, 1950.

Grandpaw had found the turtle, the large black and yellow roughback snapper, in the river silt beside one of the rotted timbers of the old locks at the Coal River picnic grounds, where the family had stopped to rest and eat before continuing on to the Old Homestead. I sat back on a large dry boulder that once had been part of the filler for the dam and held Grandpaw's red handkerchief against my bleeding nose, where shithead Hercules had just clobbered me, and I watched Grandpaw walk up and back by the timber, shading his eyes with his hand like a salute, stopping to kick lightly now and then in the mud.

"Did you whack him back?" Grandpaw asked me.

"No."

"What did you do about it then?"

"I ran, is what," I told him, and pressed the handkerchief tighter against my nose. "After I got up I did."

"You did, did you?"

"Yes, but then he ran and caught me and threw me down. He's a fat slob but he can run fast. Faster than me, anyhow. My dumb knees always knock each other when I run. But anyhow, Cynthia came up then and made him quit hitting me. And all those stupid kids down around the swings were laughing and things."

"They were? You know, my knees always had a way of stumbling me up, too. Leastways when I took out arunning. Had to learn to stand up and git it toe to toe. No chance of you doing that with Henry is they?"

"Heck no, Grandpaw. He can beat me easy every time. He can beat any of the kids on Kanawha Street. Except Cynthia, because she's nine and he's only eight. But everyone else he can beat. That's why the kids call him Hercules. On account of him being so big and all. Anyhow, Kitty says it's wrong to fight. She says you should never hurt anyone if you can help it."

"Don't get to believing everything you hear, feller. Specially from women."

Grandpaw stopped and bent over, looking squint-eyed at the ground, then took out his black bone-handled pocketknife with the nine blades. He opened the largest blade and, kneeling stiffly down, began to dig around a small copper-colored spot that shone like a dull coin through the mud haze.

"I reckon I found us something here, feller," Grandpaw said. "I figured I would. Used to be all kinds of these buggers round 'bout here."

"Should you be bending over on account of your heart, Grandpaw? Aunt Erica says you shouldn't."

"Women creatures don't know a thing," Grandpaw said.

He dug in a widening puddle, scooping the seeping water away, then began to ply under the shell until he rolled the turtle out onto its back, its yellow underside flashing suddenly bright against the dark river rocks.

"This'll take holt a body's finger and hang on it till sundown. Like a snake will. You can cut its head clean off and it'll still hang on. It just won't die off till evening time. Not till the old sun goes down. That's why you want to catch it up by its shell from the back end."

Grandpaw picked the turtle up very carefully and took it to a clear rain puddle isolated on a large boulder and flushed it around until the mud smears washed away. He brought it back then and set it on a timber near me.

"Now, there, we two got us a pet of sorts."

He took his pouch of Red Indian tobacco out of his shirt pocket and pinched a thick wad into his left jaw.

"Here you go, feller," Grandpaw said and gave me a small pinch for myself, as he often did when we were alone. "That'll ease the sting off that nose. Now don't you let any of the woman creatures catch you achewing. Hear me now?"

"Sure, I know," I told him.

Grandpaw sat down beside me and started to pare his fingernails with his knife's best honing blade. After a time, he began telling me, as he always did when we were at the Coal River Park, about the old dams and locks and about the old timey days when he was hauling on the river with his own boat. The Snakehunter. The finest boat ever.

Those days, Grandpaw would tell, when the beds of cannel bituminous coal along Coal River's banks were being worked. And several out of state concerns had come in and built a dam and locks system all the way up Coal River to Boone to make it navigable. This dam here at Coal River

Park, Grandpaw told, as he pointed out to where the old timbers and boulders piled into the river from the banks narrowing the middle channel, was number four, and was about the smallest of the lot. The locks here were only 125 by 24 feet, and had a channel depth at low water of a mere five feet or so. That didn't afford much room to spare, Grandpaw told, as the barges, the big 6,500-bushel ones, ran a good 124 by 23. Dam here had a miter sill of about twelve feet and a lock lift of nine, as I recollect it. Afforded slack water back ten miles to Petyona.

And there was no boat on this river like the old Snakehunter, Grandpaw told.

Not even the old H. E. Pierpont, with its fourteen-inch bore engines and five-foot stroke and three boilers. And all the Snakehunter was, was a hewed-out dugout from a single poplar log that had a steam engine and sidewheel bolted on. Why, they was poplar trees a good eight and ten feet in diameter around back in them days. The Olafson brothers it was that spent a full year hewing the Snakehunter out of one of them big logs. By God, was the fastest on the river and could tug well near as many barges as the big tonners. Could stay over in the shallow channels near the banks out of the hard current and that's where she come by her name. Used to brush into the willows along the banks where water snakes was stretched out sunning on the branches, and it would knock down a bushel or two full ever single trip.

When the coal played out and the locks fell to waste, Grandpaw told, we was about the only boat of any size at all what could navigate the river. Me and old Bill Trombly made a store boat out of the Snakehunter then, and went up and down the river buying and selling produce and buying ginseng and furs and hoop poles that we'd sell at Warnertown. You know what hoop poles was? Was straight-grained hickory that they used to split and bend into barrel hoops. Well, anyway, it wasn't any good anymore. Old Snakehunter was built to haul coal barges. Hauling produce wasn't no good.

We give it up before too long. The old Snakehunter finally got smashed up in the bad flooding of 1924.

Well, it was a dandy river back then days, Grandpaw said. Not much of anything now days. Not even any fishing worth anything now. Bad water killed about everything but the mudcats. And they ain't worth fishing for. Not fit for a white man to eat. Hang around sewers. Eat any and everything. Eat nigger shit.

But it was a dandy river oncet. And I remember how it was.

"I remember now too, Grandpaw," I told him. "About the river and things."

"I don't get you, feller."

"Well, you told me all these things about the river so now I can remember them too. The way you do. That way they'll stay real."

"Yes, I reckon you do remember them sort of at that. You're about the only one as seems to set any store by them."

"See, Grandpaw, I want things to remember. I don't have a whole lot of things like you and Aunt Erica do. Or like anyone. But I want a lot of them. Things, I mean."

"Well, you're welcome to 'em, scutter. They ain't exactly what a body would call practical or useful. Just old, is all."

The turtle stirred in the warm sun and started down the timber toward the green, moving water. I jumped up and chased it, then carefully picked it up from behind like Grandpaw had shown me, and carried it back up the bank. Grandpaw stood up then, slowly and stiffly, and he took the dark wet ball from his mouth and tossed it out into the river. It splashed near the first slimy hump of a sunken barge's ribs that pressed up out of the dirty water in a row, stretching into the shallow river. Catherine had once told me that these humps looked to her like the vertebrae of some old dinosaur that must have been lulled down into cool mud and water to die, and had rotted away, and now only the petrified bones thrust dark and wet from the green water. Like the fossil mammoths, I had thought. The huge creatures which had been dug from the frozen earths of Siberia and Alaska that Catherine had also told me about. Captured long ago in ice or tar and frozen for 25,000 years, she said. And once in Poland, an Ice Age woolly rhinoceros was found. As the earth changed, Catherine had told, the creatures had not. They were just fossils now. Old bones lost in the earth. Grandpaw's tobacco wad bobbed back to the surface in the stagnating water of the lee of the first hump and floated motionless. A long-legged fly flitted across the water toward it.

We heard Aunt Erica calling for us to come and eat a bite and to hurry about it. We started down the beach toward the path that led back up the hill to the picnic tables.

"How's that nose now?" Grandpaw asked.

"It's all right. You know what, Grandpaw? I didn't cry when Herk hit me. I did when I got down on the path in the trees but not when he did it where all those kids could see."

"I didn't figure you did," Grandpaw said. "I didn't figure you'd be too fast a crier. Now don't you go and forget to rinse out your mouth at that rock fountain on the path to get all the 'backy out. Don't want them creatures hollering around, do we?"

"No, we don't."

Seven

Rivers.

During the ancient Tang dynasty, the Chinese used to marry a young girl to the Yellow River once a year by drowning her in the water. The Holy Witches chose the loveliest child they could find for this fatal marriage and they conducted the ceremony themselves.

It was believed that the king of Cayor in Senegal would infallibly die within a year's time if he were to cross a river. In Mashonaland, until quite recently, the chiefs would not cross certain rivers, particularly the Rurikwi and the Nyadiri.

Catherine once read a book to me entitled *The Bengal Lancer,* in which there was a description of a rustic funeral: the funeral of a young girl. Because her relations were poor her funeral pyre was composed of green wood and so her body was not fully burned. Then, among clusters of white and yellow flowers, which are daily tribute of India's people to their water gods and goddesses, the remains of the girl were lowered into the holy river. From the midst of those drifting flowers, a seared arm rose as if it waved goodbye to the family gathered on the shore. Then it sank beneath the still water for a last time. Before long, the turtles had spotted the body and were swimming in its direction. They, like the pariah dogs and the crocodiles, were the scavengers of Juma. A large white turtle reached the body first. With a ribbon of flesh in its snapping mouth, it raised its head above the water's surface. Where the body of the girl had been, the water quickly became pale foam.

"*Sarvam Khalvidam Brahman,*" these people say. "All this is indeed God."

The Red Ash Burial Fund was organized by local miners in 1922, with dear old Grandpaw serving as its first secretary-treasurer. He was also chairman from 1924 to 1929 of the White Race Pall Bearers. There were five other miners besides himself who were also elected to serve as pallbearers, all receiving day wages equivalent to company pay for their services. The burial fund paid also for their travel expenses to the place of interment and for the opening and closing of the grave at each funeral. Altogether, the fund would pay as much as four hundred dollars and the cost of the transportation of the corpse and coffin up to four hundred miles. According to my Grandpaw, the most inaccessible burial ground was the one located on Red Ash Island, which for some reason was the place a lot of the miners chose to be planted. First the body of the deceased had to be shipped from Rush Run to Red Ash by passenger train. Then the six pall-bearers had to carry the coffin for several hours over very rough terrain. Finally, it had to be rowed through hard current to the isolated island. Grandpaw said that he had mixed feelings about being selected as a White Race Pall Bearer. It was a privilege, in one sense, to be singled out by your friends and by the men you worked with to carry their remains at the last and to take part in their funerals. There was a certain trust in that. And, also, something like an implied belief that you would be alive when they were no longer. On the other hand, there was an aspect of servitude involved, like having to do a favor you damn well knew wouldn't be paid back. And perhaps there was even the hidden wish to taint you with the touch, the shame of death. But in any case, a man received a day's wages and did not have to go into the mines to earn it. That was something anyway, Grandpaw said. Why so many chose to be buried on the isolated island he said he did not know. Maybe because it was so off to itself and peaceful. Actually, even he would have not minded to be buried there, Grandpaw said. Except that it was no longer possible. The grounds were closed in the early 1930s, after heavy flooding one spring washed open a number of the graves and sent their contents floating down the river.

Isabel, Aunt Erica's colored maid, once told Cynthia and me that after death, spirits would haunt among the flood-washed roots of the trees along river banks. We believed her. We made ourselves believe her; it was the most interesting prospect for after-death that we had heard. And we made plans based upon this belief. We decided that when at last one of us died, the survivor would go to the trees along the river and there wait for the ghost of the other to show up. We even picked out a special tree, and after Cynthia had to stay in bed all the time, we spent a great deal of effort in com-piling a "haunt list," containing all the names of those peo-ple who, in our opinion, needed to have the shit scared out of them. Sometimes we would argue about the position of priority certain names should have. Usually, however, we agreed wholeheartedly with one another.

Catherine and I walked far up the beach past the third jetty and then she pointed under the old tugboat pier which went far out over the river and told me that that was one place they lived. But I did not see any trolls. You have to go back under there, she said, if you ever want to see one. But I did not go back under. They are afraid of daylight just like vampires, she said, because it makes them curl up dead like salt on a worm, and so you always have to go back in the dark to see them. But I did not go back in the dark under the pier. Trolls did not make that much of a difference to me. It had nothing to do with the dark though, I told Catherine.

I waited until Aunt Hilda had walked partway down toward the river, then I followed behind her, holding as deep within the trees' shade as I could. She stopped at the top of the bank's rise and stationed herself with her fists curled at her hips, looking down toward the lower water where

Cynthia stood stripped to underpants thigh-deep. Hercules, whose pants' bottoms were rolled to his knees, stood in the shallows nearer the shore.

"Boy, are you in for it!" Hercules called to Cynthia when he spotted his fat mother's presence. "I told her not to do it, Mom," he called to Aunt Hilda, who had not moved.

"Just wait till your Aunt Erica spots you," Hilda called down to Cynthia. "I wouldn't want to be in your shoes, I wouldn't."

"I haven't got any shoes on," Cynthia said. "I'm standing barefoot in this wonderful water."

"Well now, aren't you the sassy cute one," Aunt Hilda said.

Cynthia just laughed and splashed her hands around in the water. Her fine blond hair, which was nearly white, looked almost luminous in the sunlight, and the ropes of current about her pale legs glazed shuddering with moving brightness. I suddenly felt from within myself a strange insistent coiling toward the water. I quickly shut my eyes. I stood very still. Everything had fallen so silent except for the flowing sound of the water. Then, pressing through the thinness of my eyelids, the bright light began to curl itself into shapes: circling shapes, circling like those ghosts of flame we would often run weaving into the evening air with sparklers. The bright shapes spread through the tissue of my lids until, finally, I had to blink my eyes open again. They were moist and warm, and I could feel a salt sting in their corners. I forgot for a moment where I was. Then I heard Aunt Hilda calling to Cynthia.

"Well, miss smart mouth, you just get the dickens on out of there. You're set to get a good one, I'll clue you right now."

"That remains to be seen," Cynthia said, and made a face at Aunt Hilda; then, splashing water again at her sides, she said to Hercules: "I know how to swim eight strokes. Do you want to see me do it?"

Hercules looked up the bank to his mother and grinned, but said nothing.

"You know you're not supposed to get your face wet with old dirty river water!" Aunt Hilda called, shaking a finger at Cynthia.

"Watch here, Herky," Cynthia said, and splashed head-long into the current, then chopped eight shattering strokes onto the surface before stopping. She stood upright, coughing slightly, and wiped her eyes free of wet hair. Then, silently looking up toward the shore to Aunt Hilda, she just stood there, her white arms braced out like wings, balancing herself in the undertow upon the slick mossy stones. From my position on the higher bank, I could see the quivering reflection of her body and face's length spread before her as it was moved and broken, yet held gathered, by the current.

"Try for ten this time!" I called to Cynthia, more surprised at my own voice than even those who heard, and who turned, looking up at me in unison. Then Cynthia waved to me and called:

"You just watch. I'll do even more than that."

She spread her thin arms above her head; then, clasping her hands in a diver's grip, she rose on tiptoes and hovered there as though waiting for the exact pulse of current. Then she dove suddenly forward, the water shedding her back like a skin of sparks. This time her strokes were more even, seeming to unfold into the very shape of the flowing water, her arms growing into the motion itself. She's doing this good for me, I thought, and watched the accumulating performance of her strokes—six, seven, eight, nine, ten—with love for her, and gratitude. Eleven, twelve, thirteen, fourteen—as though she was started on her way to the sea.

Rivers contd.

As noted before, the town of Century is located in south-ern West Virginia on the Kanawha River. This is a river of some interest to me; it is an ancient river. With only a few deviations, this river flows today as it flowed in Paleozoic times. Indeed, of all those streams that millions of years ago flowed westward from Appalachia to empty into a now ex-tinct inland sea, only the Kanawha retains something near to its original channel and direction. The name "Kanawha" was taken from a tribe of Indians, the Conoys, and was given between 1760 and 1770. For many years there was a great variety in the spelling of this name. Wyman's map of the British Empire in 1771, calls it the "Great Conoway." Daniel Boone, in his survey in 1791, spelled it "Conhaw-way."

Cynthia and I followed Lester down the dirt road be-tween the rows of small, unpainted frame houses. He cut into the narrow yard between two of the houses, leading us toward the back where there was clothing hanging on a long, sagging line in the afternoon sun. A fat colored woman was rocking in an old green glider on one of the back porches while she peeled potatoes.

"Where you headin' at, Lester Washington?" she called as we passed by her. She was watching Cynthia's face.

"I'm headin' down to the river."

"You go playing down around that old river and I bet you end up with a whipping."

"I ain't gettin' whupped by nobody," Lester said with a sneer.

We waded through the high weeds down the bank to where a line of willows traced the water's edge.

"He gonna do it right down there," Lester said, point-ing to a small sloping beach that was strewn with rubbish.

"The scene of the crime," Cynthia said and laughed quietly.

My insides felt strange, as though something was thawing from my throat and dripping into my stomach where it spread cool and warm at once.

Sammy, Lester's big brother, put them in a brown burlap sack. He put them in one at a time, first holding each up close before his eyes, looking it carefully over: looking for an extra long time into its small closed face. Seven kittens in all. One of them was pale yellow, almost the color of Cynthia's hair. Another was black. As black as Lester's face. We knelt back in the shade of the trees and quietly watched Sammy begin to dip the sack into the river. He was on his knees in the mud at the water's edge and small, dark river waves splashed up on his legs. He kept dunking the sack in and out. Strange little movements pressed out against the wet cloth sides, as though the sack was breathing. Sammy opened the sack, looking down into it for a moment, then he started to dip it in and out again while trying to hold the top open so that he could watch. But he leaned too far out and almost dropped it, so he clenched the top closed again and continued dunking until at last it hung limp and dripping.

Sammy stood up slowly. He opened the sack's top again, looking into it for a long time, jiggling it now and then, watching closely. Why is he frowning? I wondered. And the sweat. Heavy beads were across his forehead and shining in thin streams over his face and down his skinny neck. Sammy put the sack down at his feet, then slowly unbuttoned his damp shirt. He took it off and tossed it into some nearby scrub brush. He picked the sack up and walked over to a thick willow that leaned heavily far out over the river. There was no breeze, I noticed. And everything was so quiet.

Sammy began to swing the sack over his head and then against one of the tree's large, flood-washed roots with dull thuds. He swung from the right side, then the left side, then again the right. Again and again. The silence in between became sudden. The moment quiets between the thuds. A quiet moment, then again a thud like a faraway drum. Quiet. Thud. Quiet. Thud. Again and again. What the shit is he doing? I wondered. Could the kittens still be alive? But still, why do that to them? Even if the water hadn't drowned them, why hit them on a tree like he wanted to hurt them some more and break them up? Little kittens, I thought, remembering the yellow one. I felt Cynthia's arm go around my shoulders and I saw that Lester's mouth hung wide open.

Then the thuds started to sound sort of wet.

Instead of bouncing back at a hit, the sack began to smother liquidlike around the root shape. There was still no other sound. No wind. Sammy's breath, though. It began to press into the quiet moments, pushing the heavy suddenness away between the wet thuds. And his eyes were closed. He could miss the tree and fall down with his eyes shut like that, I thought, and wished he would do just that. Then started the grunts with the breath until they moved the silent moments completely away, until the thuds and grunts came together, their edges coiled into the same suddenness.

Then Sammy fell.

I knew it, I thought. I had hoped he would.

Sammy tossed over onto the brown dirty sand, the sack under his narrow chest, and the silence came rushing back. Then I heard a paddlewheel sound its whistle far down the river as it approached the locks at Deep Water and the locks sounded in return. Sammy lay in the sand.

"Let's git," Lester whispered.

"Not on your life," Cynthia said under her breath, whispering as though we were in church.

Then Sammy sat up. He slowly opened the sack and looked in it, but he kept his face back away from the lip, as though he thought something might leap out at him. He started to reach slowly into the sack but then suddenly jerked his hand away. Sammy jumped up and swung the sack over his head, tossing it far out over the water where it splashed into the middle current and disappeared.

"They's as dead as doornails," Lester whispered.

"How did you ever figure that out?" Cynthia said.

"How come Sammy did that stuff to the kittens?" I asked Cynthia.

"Who knows. Maybe he's crazy or something."

An early evening chill settled off the air of the river and I figured that it must be close to supper time. After a short while Cynthia and I trotted home.

Eight

Four-Pole Creek's water was swift and clear and it boiled about the smooth, colored rocks in the bright shallows. At least it's not up too high to ford this spring, Aunt Erica said. The spring before the creek had been running high and brown, washing up over the sloping banks into the lower trees, and I had seen a drowned swollen hog caught among some branches. We had had to park on the near side and cross on the log footbridge to Whitfield land, and the cars had been broken into by "some of that white trash," as Aunt Erica put it, who lived in tar paper shacks along the west ridge of the hollow.

"The cars always seem safer on the other side," Aunt Erica said, observing the surprisingly low water line. "On Whitfield land. Even when we can't get up the hill to the house. It's like all that trash knows better than to come onto Whitfield land."

"Still scared," Grandpaw said. "And it's been well near to thirty years since a Whitfield has shot anyone back up these bottoms. And that was when Uncle Clemson shot a preacher and Cousin Carson Hayhurst shot a government man all in the same week."

"Good lands to gracious," Aunt Erica said. "How you run on at the mouth, you old bird you."

Uncle Charlie, who was ahead of us (Grandpaw and Catherine and I were riding with Aunt Erica), drove his pickup truck down the rutted incline into the creek water and bumped, splashing, slowly across. Cynthia and Hercules, riding in the back bed with the tools and James' stone, slid with the sway, bumping against one another and laughing. I had wanted to ride back there with them and everyone had said it was all right. Everyone except Aunt Erica. I hated her guts right then. Naturally that turdhead Hercules was making faces at me.

"Gracious, am I glad we stopped at the Coal River Park," Aunt Erica said as she pulled her Plymouth to a halt, waiting for Uncle Charlie to cross the creek. "What with Albert's and Tom's tribes here this year, Julia and Garnet will have more than enough to feed and tend to. Neither of them is too well these days, you know."

"None of us is too well these days," Catherine said.

"Well, it surely does seem sometimes like just everyone has gotten so old all of a sudden," Aunt Erica said, then continued, "Kitty, do you know what's been ailing Mary Jane these days? Has she said anything to you at all?"

"Why, no she has not," Catherine said. "Should she have?"

"Well, something just isn't right, is all. I've caught her and Hilda whispering around like a couple of schoolgirls about something several times."

"Well, I can't imagine," Catherine said. "I haven't heard anything at all. Of course, Mary Jane wouldn't confide in me anyway, I don't expect. After the way I've been ribbing her about her beau."

"Well, something is amiss."

"It beats me. Besides, it's none of my business," Catherine said, and took her medicine bottle from her large, straw-thatched purse: the one she had brought back from her Mexican tour two summers ago, along with the weird Aztec masks that hung in her room and the clusters of beads and the Indian arrowheads which she had given to me. The things she brought back in lieu of a loverboy, she had declared. She took a deep drink from her medicine bottle, then burped, and gave me a big wink.

"Don't you dare start that stuff today!" Aunt Erica said.

"Auntie, dear, you may raise all the holy hell you wish with the rest of the quaking family," Catherine said. "But you should certainly know better after all these years than to light in on me. I have as many mean bones in my deceptively frail frame as you do in your chicken-muscled torso. So do not tread. We are of the same cast, Auntie."

"You talk too much, Catherine Whitfield," Aunt Erica said.

She hunched forward clutching the steering wheel until her hands, high on the wheel, stretched white over her knuckles and the brown splotches paled vanilla with tautness. She twisted the wheel with jerks as she started down the bank, her elbows held wide and high, the left one knocking an erratic beat against the door. She bumped her Plymouth out into the bright, moving creek. I could feel the flush and pushing of the water; and when I shut my eyes, just listening to the splashing sounds, I even felt a little dizzy, as though the car was being floated away, around and around in the current like a cellophane candy wrapper in a rainy gutter or one of my shells swirling on the streaming kitchen linoleum.

Grandpaw began to jerk at the rear window's handle, trying to lower it.

"This thing still won't get down properly," he said.

"Clint, if you're fixing to spit out that window, just don't you do it!" Aunt Erica told him. "I said to use that coffee can I cleaned out for you. Why do you think I brought it? You spitting tobacco wads out the car window like a cow heaving over a fence is downright sickening!"

"Spittin' in a can ain't spittin' at all. That's slobbin' is what that is. Runs down my chin onto my shirt front is what that does," Grandpaw said, and hocked deep in his throat like a toilet flush and spit.

Grandpaw was the best spitter of anyone I ever knew, including Catherine. He could sit on Aunt Erica's front porch and spit all the way to the first elm, almost always hitting the small cement-filled knothole even though he had to wear a dark green glass over the left lens of his bifocals because of his cataracts. It just takes practice and determination to make a good spitter, Grandpaw always said, but a great spitter is another color of horse completely. It has to be in the blood. And Whitfields have it. All Whitfields who have wanted to be and worked at it, Grandpaw told, are great spitters.

"Oh, that's just so nasty," Aunt Erica said. "I should of left you back home, you old bird."

Uncle Charlie had pulled his truck up and parked where the narrow dirt road that led to the house suddenly slanted steep to the right and coiled up out of the hollow like a snake through the wooded hills. Cynthia and Hercules had already jumped down from the truck bed and run back to the creek's edge. They kicked and splashed water at us as we pulled near the bank. Hercules was still making faces and I decided right then and there that somehow today I was going to pull something on him. Maybe I could figure out a way to get Cynthia to beat him up, I calculated. Or maybe I could get some grownup to whip him.

"Do you see Herk making all those faces at me, Aunt Erica?"

"Pay him no mind."

"But he's been doing it all day long. And he hit me in the nose back at the park."

"Well, just hit him back. Quit whining around so much."

Strike one.

Aunt Erica almost spun her Plymouth's left rear wheel into a mudhole at the creek's edge, but gave a sudden hard press of gas that lunged the car up the bank, spraying rocks and water everywhere, and sent Hercules and Cynthia scampering. The quick movement threw me forward almost against the dashboard. It caused Grandpaw to swallow his tobacco and he started choking and coughing.

Aunt Erica pulled the car up the road about fifty yards then turned left off onto a cleared hard sand area that was in the deep shade of a large shagbark hickory. Uncle Albert's and Uncle Tom's cars were already there, parked back out of the sun in the shaded coolness, and Aunt Erica pulled beside them as deep into the darkness as she could. Uncle Charlie walked over to us from his truck.

"Well, what now?" he asked Aunt Erica. "Do we just sit around and wait for Mary Jane and her boyfriend to catch up?"

"They ought to be coming along right away," Aunt Erica said. "Don't go getting your dander up. Let's get some of the picnic leftovers out of my trunk and into your truck. Where is Hilda?"

"Did you see him pull off or something?" Uncle Charlie asked. "I thought he was right behind you."

"No, I did not," Aunt Erica said. "They'll be along directly. I asked you where your wife was."

"Still flopped in the truck I guess."

Grandpaw was still coughing from his swallowed tobacco and Catherine was pounding him on the back.

"Clint, will you kindly stop all that racket!" Aunt Erica told him. "That hooping around just makes me sick to my stomach."

Grandpaw kept right on coughing, but he looked up at Aunt Erica through tear-wet eyes and shook his head as though in disbelief.

"I hope we don't have to sit around here in this hot sun for long," Hilda called from the truck. She was still sitting in the cab and was fanning herself with a magazine.

"They'll be right along," Aunt Erica called back. "Hilda, why don't you come over here in the shade. Get out of that hot truck. I've got something to talk to you about anyway."

"Well, bugs is always so thick back in tree shade," Hilda said. "Lands, I just feel awful."

"Well, you come on over here," Aunt Erica said. "I want to talk to you."

"I feel rather poorly also," Catherine said. "I am planning to get the devil out of this three-dollar girdle. My poor flesh is squeezing right through the little holes."

Hilda walked slowly over to the car. The straps of her brassiere were out of line with her sundress straps, and they curled up along their edges as they dug into her damp white skin. Small blue broken veins looked like ink etch marks on her upper chest.

"Well, Kitty, just think if that pretty bachelor friend of Uncle Albert's from the state legislature isn't here today after all," Hilda said. "All that squeezing hot rubber misery for nothing."

"Well, bachelor or not," Catherine said, "I'm about prepared to wiggle it off and just take my fading chances puffed out in the natural. Wearing a girdle for me is like wearing a five-and-dime Halloween mask and going trick-treating on Christmas."

Aunt Erica had opened the car's trunk and she stood back by the rear fender.

"Hilda, come on back here with me for a minute," she said.

"I brought a half a can of Crisco shortening, Kitty," Hilda said. "So if you need a good greasing to help you peel it off, you're welcome to use some."

Hilda thrust her chin high and forward and wiped her damp handkerchief up her neck. The sweaty grime beaded from the stretched flesh rolls like thin dark strings.

"But if you take it off," Hilda said, "you won't be tricking sure enough. And like as not treating."

"Hilda, I've got something to ask you," Aunt Erica said. "Now come on back here."

"You don't need a girdle anyway, honey," Hilda said. She leaned heavily against the car. Her eyes were dark from her sweat-smeared mascara. "Lands, Kitty, you are as spare as a bird. I take back what I said about you not getting to do some trick-treating if you take that girdle off."

"Unfortunately I have a beer gut that pops out like I was six months gone," Catherine said.

"And whose fault is that?" Aunt Erica said. She walked back around from the car's rear. "We have a few things left to transport to Charlie's truck."

"Well, honey, don't expect much from me," Hilda said. "I'm about weltered away."

"Hilda, I'll tell you exactly what I expect from you," Aunt Erica said. "You tell me what Mary Jane has up her sleeve. What have you two been whispering around about. I know good and well there is something going on."

"Well, honey, I swand if I know what you're talking about."

"What is it now! Why has she been mooning around and all? I'm not blind, you know."

"For heaven's sake," Hilda said. "You do beat all."

Hilda pushed heavily from the car's fender, leaving a damp imprint from the wet back of her dress, and headed for the path that Hercules and Cynthia had run down toward the creek bank.

"I'm going to get those kids out of that creek," Hilda said.

"We'll just see," Aunt Erica said. "We'll just see about this whole thing."

"What are you going on about anyway?" Uncle Charlie asked.

"That's what you get, Charlie, for marrying a cheap dime store clerk," Aunt Erica told him.

"What the devil are you carrying on about?"

"We'll just see."

Catherine was sitting beside Grandpaw on the rear fender of Aunt Erica's Plymouth.

"Let's you and I explore this surrounding wilderness,"

she called to me. "We might find ourselves a dandy place to homestead or something."

"Sure," I told her.

"Marvelous. Marvelous. Well, let us shake a leg," she said, getting up from the fender, stretching and yawning, then walking slowly toward the dirt road that led away from the creek crossing.

"Grandpaw, will you watch out for my turtle?" I asked, running over to where he was sitting.

"Where is it, feller?"

"I put it in a box in the back of Uncle Charlie's truck."

"Well, I'll keep an eye peeled out."

"I thought up a name for it, Grandpaw. It's secret though. Let me whisper it to you."

"Well, don't slobber in my ear," he said, bending over a little.

I whispered the secret name to him.

"That's a dandy name, all right," he said.

"Yeah. And we can signal about it. Like we got a secret club with a secret password or something. We'll say 'S and H' when we talk about it. Okay?"

"Good enough, scutter."

"Come on, Dick Tracy, if you are coming," Catherine called to me.

She was over by Uncle Charlie's truck and I could see heat waves quivering up into the bright air from its hood right behind her.

"Wait up," I called, and ran to catch her. When I passed the truck I took a quick peek at my turtle. Its weird green head was out of its shell peering about, confused by the strange cardboard world around it.

Catherine and I followed the dirt road as it paralleled the creek's course up the narrow bottoms. I tried to walk balanced on the crusted ridge between two deep ruts. A few steps around a slight bend, out of sight of the truck and cars, we entered a wood of holly and birch which rose in thick clumps on either side of the road. The sunlight through the thick summer leaves looked strange as it dabbled gently over Catherine's shadowed face. When we had passed through the trees I noticed a couple of sets of old railroad tracks to my left across the creek. They were grown over with dark tangling vines and brush. A pile of unused tie timber lay off to one side and was covered with moss and small blue flowers. Further up the tracks were two old coal cars, forgotten and vacant, rusting in dull yellow webs out from the bolt heads that riveted like marching lines of helmets up their sides.

"I simply can't abide empty containers," Catherine said, imitating Aunt Erica's voice, and making a little gesture toward the coal cars. "It is a holy, moral, practical obligation to fill up empty containers."

We both laughed. But I couldn't help thinking of Catherine's own cans and jars. The rows and rows of them, along with the clay flowerpots and glass vases, that crammed the floor to ceiling shelves of the glassed-in back porch of Aunt Erica's house. They were filled with earth, dark and rich, and with stick stems of flowers with impossible names. And they were packed in their ordered lines tight enough to darken the light from the broad windows with heavy criss-crossing shadows.

—I can't see why you waste your time with all them sticks, Kitty, Aunt Hilda often said.

The flowers never seemed to bloom, or at best seldom. And there was the one kind that Catherine always sat up to watch on the single night of each year when it spread its few moments of color. It was like waiting up to catch Santa Claus or the Easter Bunny, Catherine would say. Twice I had tried to wait up to watch with her, but had fallen asleep both times. And Catherine had refused to wake me, saying that you had to stay awake all on your own or you did not deserve to witness the blossom. It was as though, Catherine would say, her gaunt little stick sucked months of the sun's warm host into its cold sap and apparently futile roots, then like a strange joke on everyone, bloomed in the black obscurity of night. But the point is, Catherine said, it does indeed bloom. However infrequent or faint, it does eventually blossom. It lives. It lives on its own terms.

Old Catherine was a real caution.

Catherine and I turned off the dirt road onto an old overgrown logging trail which we leisurely followed as it circled around the mountain, always rising, but slowly, toward the higher forests. After a time we came upon a small hillside meadow to the right of the road. It was rain gullied and thick with wild wheat and spring field flowers.

"Well," Catherine said, "let's get our tails in gear. I see at least two million glorious flowers whose lives I must pick."

We stepped from the road onto the slope and began to move about in the high weeds, picking flowers. Small grasshoppers flicked away from our legs as we waded trenches through the stiff grass. Because I planned to take them to her, I carefully picked dear old Ma's favorites: the small, glowing, bright pinks, the yellow-eyed daisies, the tall and purple milkweeds. Catherine selected only long delicate stems of Queen Anne's lace, which seemed to swell and drip like boiling foam from her bunched cluster. We finally reached the edge of the forest where the bramble and brier bushes began to clump and were tangled about with honeysuckle and lacing buckvines. Catherine showed me how to gently pluck the small brown bead from the honeysuckle's center, then quickly but easily pull its thin string taut and taste the sweet clear liquid before it beaded and dripped. I began to follow along the brush line, picking the largest, sweetest flowers. I must have been daydreaming as I wandered along the edge of the forest, for I remember suddenly realizing how far I had moved away from Catherine across the field. She stood knee-deep in the grass and weeds exactly where we had first reached the forest, and her head was tilted back in a strange position as she silently watched the dark woods.

"What are you doing, Kitty?" I called to her.

"I am observing."

"What?"

"Something I imagined I saw."

"What?"

I started to run through the high grass toward her, keeping my eye peeled out on the woods.

"Just something I thought I saw. For a fleeting moment."

"But what? What was it?"

"Well, it was something I found to be extremely spooky."

"You're just saying that. I know your tricks."

"Indeed, I am not. I cross my heart and hope to die. I saw an old, mangy, snaggle-toothed vampire flying around under those trees."

"You did not. Vampires can't come out in the daylight."

"Come to think of it, you may be right. Actually, it was more like a plain old average ghost, I guess. I saw it, though. It was spooking its haunty heart out up on that footpath. Probably it was looking for someone to gobble up."

"Sure. I just bet it was."

"Well, it was. Cross my heart and hope to die."

"Well, I happen to know that ghosts don't come out in the daytime either."

"Well, this particular one did. It was looking for a little black-headed boy to eat for a snack, I betcha."

"It was not either."

"Oh yes it was."

"You're just trying to scare me. I know you. You didn't see anything up there."

"Oh yes I did. I even recognized the ghost."

"Who is it then?"

"A certain Miss Catherine Whitfield, that's who."

"You mean you?"

"Yes, indeed. I mean me all right. Well, about a twenty-year-old me at any rate."

"I don't know what you mean."

"Well, Dick Tracy, I thought I glimpsed a young me going up that old footpath. And there was a mild autumn breeze stirring my hair and leaves were red and golden. And as the air shifted softly around and around, all those beautiful dead leaves just kept falling and falling and falling. And I thought how beautiful it must be to be dead and falling so gently like that."

"I don't see. I don't know what you mean at all."

"Oh, dear, it is just foolish pretend. Like a daydream, that's all."

Catherine put her fingers into my hair and smiled down at me. With her other hand she patted my cheek. Her hand smelled strange. The hair on her arms was damp with sweat and looked dark. The hair on her upper lip was damp and dark also.

"Well, I still don't see."

"Well, Dick Tracy, it is somewhat nutty, which is par for the course for me. And nutty things have a perverse tendency to be difficult to explain."

From the large front pocket of her brightly striped dress Catherine took out her medicine bottle. She took two quick drinks, then ran her tongue over her upper lip.

"What were you doing on that path anyway?"

"Just starting up it," Catherine said, her voice very quiet and strange, like it was sometimes. "It was a shortcut to an old sandstone quarry that W.P.A. workers hewed out of the cliffs up that ridge, back during the thirties. I used to go up there with a friend when I was in college to look for fossils. It was a fine place to fossil hunt all right. The rocks were extremely well exposed and weathered. I came across some dandy prints up there. Some of the best I have ever seen anywhere. You know, the ones I have deposited in the top drawers of the collection chest."

"Who was your friend?" I asked. "The one who went up there with you to the quarry."

"Just a friend. A pimply-faced friend with terribly thick glasses. And with ears that stuck out like a taxi coming around the corner with its doors wide open."

Catherine took another drink from her bottle.

"Your friend sounds real ugly."

"Indeed he was. He certainly was. Quite awful, I suppose. When he would perspire his bumps would open and seep. How endearing that was. By the by, he was the blackguard who initiated me into our favorite hobby, yours and mine. Our fossils. He was in my junior geology lab and it was intense love over a spectroscope. Your Grandpaw had told me about the old quarry, so here we came. At my suggestion, of course. We came only a few times, actually, that autumn. During Indian summer. Four or five times, I guess. That's all."

"Did you say you loved him?"

"Did I say that? Why, you must be mistaken."

"I think you said that."

"What with all those boisterous bumps of his?"

"Did you ever kiss him?"

"Well now, I will simply have to confess the whole sordid affair. Because I did try to kiss him now and then. But more often than not I would miss his mouth completely and kiss a bump. As a matter of fact his mouth looked an awfully lot like a bump. Funny pursed thing, that mouth."

"Ugh."

"Indeed, ugh."

"What was his name?"

"Oscar."

"That's really a funny name."

"Certainly is. Poor Oscar was such a romantic. For someone with so many bumps, anyway. He used to babble about fossils as though they were fused with some sort of magical manna potency or something."

"What does that mean?"

"Oh, honey, just magic. That's all. Magic. Magic."

Softly, under her breath, Catherine began to hum, and then to sing. And taking my hands in hers, we began to move around and around the hillside in slow circles as she sang. The high weeds whipped against my legs. We began to go faster. She sang faster. She sang:

under a juniper tree   juniper tree
the bones sang   the bones sang
scattered and shining   scattered and shining

As though through water, I moved, my steps too high and heavy and too slow. I fell down. Catherine held fast to my hands and pulled me swinging to my feet again.

"You made me fall down!"

"Poor, poor little thing."

"I don't like to fall down. My legs are going to itch now from the grass."

"Well, I will help you scratch the itchy itch."

"What were you doing all that for, anyway? I don't like to hop around."

"It was a moment of mere madness. I am, I fear, a screwball. Alas, I have been into my tonic a bit too much and this spring weather really grabs an old doll like myself."

"Well, whatever happened to Oscar in the end? Where is he now?"

"Well, Dick Tracy, odd Oscar and I found many, many fine fossils. I earned an A in the class. He earned a B. On June 10th of the following summer, in a lovely candlelight ceremony, he married a certain Joyce Snyder. She had been my roommate for a couple of years. I was a bridesmaid. Joyce had her share of bumps also."

"Let's you and me go up to that place sometime. That quarry."

"Well, I doubt if we could now. It is all overgrown. And I

have been told that it is a regular copperhead den these days."

"We don't want to go up there then, do we? Who wants to get snake bit?"

"We certainly don't. Not us guys."

"Only I sure would like to see some places like that sometime that has funny things."

"Oh I know of lots of joints with funny things. There are lots of joints we can go to. This old doll has been to more than a few joints in her time."

"Like where? Tell me some of them."

"Well, let me see. Over at Hunghart's Creek Falls there is a petrified root which is quite a curiosity. The shale has worn away from the fall of the water and has exposed what was once a tree root. And all over its surface are pieces of glistening stone which look exactly like staring eyes. They seem to look right straight at you. And you can move to the left or right and those eyes will always seem to follow. They look at you as though they know your very name and have known it from the beginning of time."

"That's scary."

"Indeed. Scary as hell."

"Scary as hell. Scary as hell."

"That is exactly what I say. I could not agree with your profound appraisal more."

"Scary as hell. Scary as hell."

"What? I just realized what you said. I cannot believe my own two ears. Where did you pick up such vulgar words? Where did you lose your innocence? Such language from a mere child! A lamb, no less!"

"Well, I even know worse words than 'hell.' I've known them for a long time. I even know how to make a dirty sound. Cynthia told it to me."

"I simply cannot bring myself to believe it. Nice little children like I have attempted to raise you up to be do not even know such words exist. I must have failed. Somewhere I have failed."

"Just listen to this," I told her.

"I simply can't bear it. I feel faint. My own child."

I slipped my hand into my shirt and cupped it under my armpit. Then, quickly, I flopped my arm up and down, up and down, until the sound squeezed out. The awful wet sound. But funny wet because, when they did it, Cynthia and Hercules always laughed like hell. I kept pumping my arm making the wet awful sound and I told Catherine:

"Juicy fart   Juicy fart   Juicy fart."

Catherine slapped one hand to her mouth. Her other hand she slapped against her forehead. Her eyes rolled up into her head and she fell backward softly into the high grass and lay there moaning.

"You better get up or I'll kick you!"

"I've failed," she moaned.

I jumped on top of her and sat straddled across her stomach. She became very quiet then, and let her head roll to one side.

"You're just playing dead. I know your tricks."

Catherine was so very still. From the deep woods high up the mountain, a woodpecker's steady even rapping resounded like a distant drum. All else was quiet.

"Okay, the game's over. Quit playing dead."

Catherine was absolutely still. She was not even breathing.

I pulled up handfuls of the stiff grass and rubbed it in her face and on her neck.

"Yipes! Help! Someone save me!"

"Just for playing dead I'm going to hold you prisoner in this grass."

"But my family! My tiny children! My handsome husband! Who will wash his stinking socks?"

"I'll let you up only if you make me a promise."

"Anything, master! Anything!"

"Will you swear you and me will go to all those places with funny things?"

"Oh yes, I certainly will. I will take you just anywhere you have an inclination or need to go. I swear it. I cross my heart and hope to die."

Catherine reached up to put her hand on my cheek again. It still smelled strange.

Nine

Snakes.

A young girl told of a dream she had in which a snakelike monster with many horns kills and devours all the other animals in the world. But then God comes from the four corners, being in fact four separate gods, and gives rebirth to all the animals.

As Moses lifted up the serpent in the wilderness, even so must the Son of man be lifted up.

When a Cherokee has dreamed of being stung by a snake, he is treated just in the same way as if he had really been stung. Otherwise, the place would swell and ulcerate in the usual manner, though perhaps years later. It is, you see, the ghost of a snake that has bitten him in sleep.

The nineteenth century German chemist, Kekule, researching into the molecular structure of benzene, dreamed of a snake with its tail in its mouth. He interpreted the dream to mean that the structure of the molecule was a closed carbon ring. This was correct.

The Warramunga of central Australia believe in a formidable but mythical snake called the Wollunqua, which lives in a pool. When they speak of it among themselves they designate it by another name. They say that were they to call the snake too often by its real name, they would lose control over the creature, and it would come up out of the water and devour them.

Of all the family, Catherine wrote only to me during the time she was dying in the sanitarium. Her letters were weird, naturally. She would never write about what she was doing or how she was getting along or anything like that. Instead, she just told me strange little stories. It took me a long time to figure them out. Years, sometimes. Some of them I have never figured out.

Far away in another land, a land, Catherine wrote, of groves of mango and bright strange birds, there exist various rules about the proper building of houses: rules which are of a religious nature and which must be closely followed if a builder wishes to have luck with his house so that it will be secure and last for a long time. The first and most important of these rules is that before the builder sets by his own hand, as prescribed, the first stone of his house, he must consult the science of a religious man—an astrologer in this case. Now, it is the work of this astrologer to search about the planned foundation of the house until he divines with his magic the exact spot above the head of that snake which supports our world. From the wood of the Khadira tree the builder then carves a sharpened stake and at the divined spot above the snake's head he hammers this prepared wood deep into the ground. The snake's head is fastened securely by this action, and is a primal gesture of colonization; for if ever this snake should shake its head violently free, our world would fly like a shower of swirling birds to pieces. The builder rests his cornerstone, then, always at the center of the world, and because of this, everything is forever secure as when in the beginning Indra smote the Serpent in its lair, his thunderbolt's brightness severing the snake's head for the first time.

Snake Road.
It was called Snake Road and it had been falling apart for years, its narrow, chuckhole-pocked pavement twisting up through the wooded hills south of town seeming to go no-where at all, just circling through the hills turning back and back on itself. According to the local story, the road had been started many years before by work gangs of prisoners from the state penitentiary; then, later on in the 1930s, it had been worked on some more by federal W.P.A. laborers. Why it was started in the first place and just where it was

supposed to go, no one seemed to remember for sure, at least no one I ever talked to about it. For many years this road had been the town's main lovers' lane, where at least a couple of generations of high school kids had gone up to knead their love in parked cars at night. It was also the place where the even younger kids of the town went to learn their own early lessons about love: went to hide behind trees and bushes beside the road, hoping to catch a glimpse of the mystery through steamed-up car windows.

I saw my very first used rubber beside this road. I saw it on a warm spring Sunday afternoon when I was about eight or nine years old. I was tagging along with that gang of older guys whose ranks I was forever trying to penetrate, the one led by Hutch, the tough dude (this was some time before I blasted him in the face with that branch in that tunnel), and we had been hiking around all morning in the hills above town when we emerged from the woods onto the old road. Although this was my first encounter with the road, the older guys had been there many times before and they knew just what to look for. I acted like I knew just what to look for too, but I didn't know, really. When they found the used rubber I acted like I knew exactly what was going on, exactly what the big deal was all about. When the rest of the guys started punching each other and snickering I punched and snickered right along with them. When they started kicking the used rubber around the road I gave it a couple of kicks too. Then Hutch picked the used rubber up with a stick and tossed it at one of the other guys. Then everyone got sticks and started picking it up and tossing it at each other, dodging it and laughing like crazy. Once, Hutch had given it a really high toss and it had come down on top of my head. I had screamed and shook my head violently to get it off. Everybody fell down on the ground laughing. I laughed too, just as loud as I could.

When we got tired of tossing the used rubber around we started searching along on the sides of the road for other interesting things that people had left behind. Down over a bank Hutch had discovered a pair of girl's panties. They were light blue cotton and there were brownish stains on them. Hutch said that the stains were dried blood which meant that some pussy had lost her cherry here. I didn't know exactly what Hutch meant by this, but the strange combination of the light blue panties and the dried bloodstains with cherries spun fantastic images in my weird head, and the instantly recalled taste of cherry juice was keen in my mouth as I pictured blood coming from a girl's body being soaked up in light-blue cotton.

When we finally got ready to head back for home, Hutch picked the used rubber up again with a short stick. He told the rest of the guys that he had a good plan for it back in the neighborhood. They would get a million more laughs out this old rubber yet, Hutch told everyone. He gave the stick with the rubber to me to carry and he told me to try to keep it out of sight. He told me that if a cop saw me with it I could get sent up the river. When everybody laughed, I did too. I didn't like the idea of carrying that thing around on a stupid stick at all, but I knew that the price you paid for getting to hang out with older guys was to do the punk-kid dirty work. We took all the back routes we could on our way home, and nobody spotted me with the used rubber. When we finally got back to the neighborhood, we buried the rubber in the needle loam under a small pine tree in my back yard. The plan was to meet under the streetlight at the corner after dinner, like we were going to play kick-the-can just as usual.

I didn't really have anything against old Miss Frazier. Some of the older guys had had her for their sixth grade teacher and they said that she was a regular shit. Also, Uncle Charlie had once called her a sour old biddy after she had had the two sugar maples in her front yard cut down because, she said, she didn't like being bothered with sweeping the leaves off her porch all the time in the fall. On one Halloween I had written FUCK with soap on her front window as a part of my ever-continuing initiation into the older guys' gang. It had been Hutch's idea, of course. I had not been all that sure about what the word meant but I knew how to spell it and that was all that mattered.

We met under the streetlight after dinner as planned and played kick-the-can until it grew dark. Then Hutch told us the deal. I had to do all the dirty work, of course. First I had to go unbury the used rubber and then, after I had made it back to where the gang was waiting, I found that Hutch was all ready with another shitty job for me to do. I had to actually touch that dirty old used rubber with my fingers. I had to hold it open while Hutch poured some milk into it from a small bottle he had swiped at his home earlier. This would make it look more gooey and slimy, like some old nigger had used it, Hutch said and everyone snickered, including me, although I didn't feel much like it. While Hutch and the rest of the gang hid in the shadows of the lawn right across the street from old Miss Frazier's house, I crept up on her front porch. I was even more scared this time than when I had written FUCK with soap on her window. I was sure that she was just waiting to jump out at me from right behind her door. I saw glaring faces flash behind every dark window. A car suddenly approached from up the street, its headlights sweeping the lawns and houses. In one swirling motion I dropped the used rubber, rang the doorbell, and bolted back down the steps like a bat out of hell. I flashed like a phantom across the street just feet in front of the car, whose driver slammed on the brakes and started honking his horn. I pressed flat in the dark grass under the tree where I had rolled. In a few moments the car went on again. I could hear Hutch and the others snickering from their various hiding places around the yard. This time I didn't snicker along with them at all. I just lay there with my eyes shut and listened to the blood beat in my brain.

Old Miss Frazier didn't answer her doorbell for a long time. In fact, Hutch had just called to me to go back and ring

it again when, much to my relief, her porch light finally
clicked on. For a few moments I couldn't see old Miss Frazier
because of the silverish sheen cast on her screen door by the
porch light. Then the screen door opened slowly and old Miss
Frazier took a few hesitant steps out onto her front porch.
She was wearing a floor-length pink quilted robe with something shiny like sequins around its collar and buttonholes,
and her bluish-gray hair was brushed back to where it hung
straight and loose down her back almost to her waist. I was
surprised at the way she looked. I could never have pictured
old Miss Frazier like this. The old shit in the dark dresses with
her dull hair twisted up into tight turdlike buns on her head,
who never smiled and whose voice was always brittle and
snappish. Right now, in the bright light on the porch, she
seemed almost to glow, her girlish pink robe soft and luminous, its sequins catching light like splinters of colored glass,
and her long hair, lush with bluish highlights. Even her old
face seemed blurred and softened. Suddenly I felt very sad,
and I wasn't even sure what I felt sad about.

Old Miss Frazier had noticed the used rubber right away,
and she walked slowly up to it. Her old face puckered up into
a puzzled look and she bent way down over the used rubber,
squinting her eyes at it. Suddenly she hopped back from it
and her mouth fell open just like in a cartoon. Hutch and the
rest of the gang were snickering violently. I started snickering along with them, but not for long. Old Miss Frazier
backed up to her screen door, not taking her eyes off of the
used rubber for a moment. She opened the door and backed
on inside her house. She slammed the door and turned off her
porch light. Hutch and the rest of the gang were rolling
around in the grass pummeling each other's backs and choking on their laughter. I just sat there quietly in the dark under
the tree.

After a time, Hutch and the gang quieted down again and
they all just flopped on their backs on the lawn, exhausted
from their laughter. I lay on my back also, looking up at the

clear sky of stars. I remembered Catherine once telling me
that it had taken millions of years for starlight to flow through
empty space to our eyes, and so all the stars we thought we
were seeing here and now were really only the ghosts of stars.
That seemed so mysterious. Everything seemed so mysterious. I felt strangely, so very tired. I lay there in the cool grass
and shut my eyes and the darkness folded about me. I felt as
though I could go to sleep right then and there and that I
could sleep forever.

Then I heard old Miss Frazier come back onto her porch.
I rolled quickly over onto my stomach to watch her. She had
not clicked the porch light on this time and so through the
darkness she was only a pale form. She had a broom with her
and using short, brisk strokes she swept the used rubber off
her porch. Then she swept it down her front steps and up
her walk to the curb. The "swisk" sounds of the straw
scratched harshly on the pavement and I was sure I could
hear old Miss Frazier's breath rattling in and out with little
gasps. When she reached the curb old Miss Frazier gave the
used rubber one last big sweep out into the dark road. For a
few moments she just stood there at the curb looking around.
She was probably trying to spot one of us, I thought, and I
hugged the ground. It occurred to me that she might even
come across the street looking for us and although I knew
that I could easily outrun her, this thought filled me with a
sickening dread. But old Miss Frazier didn't move. Not for a
long time, anyway. Not until she finally just turned around
and walked slowly back into her house.

Ten

Decoration Day, 1950, contd.

When Vince pulled the black and white county sheriff's car, a new model Ford, into the creek, he switched on the siren. He splashed the car rapidly across the shallows, the water spraying high and wide on both sides. I could see Ma quickly rolling up her window and Vince laughing. The Ford bounced up the near bank, its wheels slipping and spinning, its back end fishtailing, and Vince kept laughing. His right arm rested along the seat's top and his left hand flipped casually at the steering wheel. He pulled the Ford into a space behind Aunt Erica's Plymouth, halting with a jerk just inches from her car's rear fender, then he waved broadly at the family.

"We ought to report him for using that county vehicle for personal use," Grandpaw said. "He just drove it in the first place to agitate Charlie."

"That there is a big bunch of baloney and you know it," Hilda said. "You heard Mary Jane tell that his own car is in the garage."

"Well, they's no need for blasting that sireen," Grandpaw said.

"You're just throwing down on Vince 'cause he's the one wearing that badge and not Charlie," Hilda said. "Just 'cause Vince knows how to get ahead. Now that there is yourall's thorn."

"Let it drop," Uncle Charlie said.

Ma began combing her long dark hair as Vince slid out from behind the wheel and walked around to open her door. He was a large man who I always thought looked like Victor Mature, although his features were just beginning to blur a bit with weight. He wore his sheriff khakis and there were wide, dark sweat stains under his arms. He escorted Ma toward us, his hand on the small of her back, his big teeth very white in his dark, grinning face. He whipped a handkerchief out, wiping it across his shining forehead. To me he looked like a regular greaseball, Victor Mature or not.

"Long time, no see," Ma said.

"Well, let's get this showboat back on the road," Vince said, laughing.

"We have been waiting," Aunt Erica said. "For over half an hour."

"Hey, we sure are sorry, Miss Whitfield," Vince said. "I had me a stinkin' lousy flat tire. The heaps the county gives you. Don't it figure. The dang thing popped like a bust balloon."

"Youall took your time," Aunt Erica said. "We couldn't start up the hill without the pans youall have in your trunk. You have the chicken and the macaroni salad."

"So he don't drive like a maniac like the people in this family," Hilda said.

"We told you we had a flat tire," Ma said. "Have the kids been okay? Were they any trouble or anything?"

"What the gracious is wrong with your eyes, Mary Jane?" Aunt Erica said. "They are as red as beets."

"For heaven's sake," Ma said. "Aunt Erica, you do beat all. I got too much sun at the picnic grounds. I asked about the kids."

"Kitty and me picked flowers, Ma," I told her, and handed her the ones I'd picked.

"Well, my, my. Aren't these the prettiest things you ever saw."

"Hey, there's my boy," Vince said to me. "Hey, Rocky boy. Get them dukes up, boy. Let's see the old left. C'mon Rocker, the ol' one two, one two."

"My name is Speer."

"Ah, c'mon, Rocker boy," Vince said, raising his hands into a fighter's stance, stooping and flipping his fingers lightly against my face.

"Quit it."

"Hey, ol' timer, I'm just playing, is all," Vince said. "Just kidding. Just kidding with you, little buddy."

"Don't be such a little sissy poo poo," Hilda told me.

"Hey, Sheriff, I'll fight you any ol' day," Hercules called and ran from where he and Cynthia had been digging with spoons in the dirt beside the road. He started swinging at Vince's legs.

Vince cupped Hercules' forehead in his large hand, holding him off. Hercules kept swinging wildly at Vince's legs and laughing.

"Hey, this boy is a tiger, Charlie," Vince said, laughing. "You got a regular tiger boy here."

"That's enough of that, Henry," Uncle Charlie said.

"I bet you was thinking your sister and me made off with the chest of beer, Charlie," Vince said. "How 'bout that, boy? Did you think I stole the beer?"

"The county sheriff stealing the beer," Hilda said, laughing. "That's a real corker."

"Didn't occur to me," Uncle Charlie said.

I walked around to where Catherine was standing alone in front of the truck. She was looking up the dirt road toward the woods.

"What are you doing, Kitty?"

"Nothing explainable, Dick Tracy."

"Kitty, it's not right to fight and hit, is it?"

"Let's just say that it's a waste of time."

Aunt Erica and Uncle Charlie carried several pans over to the truck from the sheriff's car.

"Well, let's get started up that old road," Aunt Erica said. "I figure we have us a little haul. It doesn't look too bad though, thank heavens."

"I just can't believe we have to walk up that dusty road," Ma said with a big sigh.

"Well, Clint Whitfield isn't," Aunt Erica said. "Now, Clint, you get yourself in and ride with Charlie."

"I cut me a walking stick here and I'm asettin' out," Grandpaw said.

"You old bird you, you haven't got one lick of sense."

"Well, I'm riding if no one else is or not," Hilda said. "I'd be a goner long before I ever got up that hill."

"Not sure the truck can haul both you and that heavy stone up the hill," Uncle Charlie said.

Vince slapped his knee, laughing.

"Oh good Lord, Hilda," Vince said. "You gonna let the old man get away with that?"

"He's not getting away with a thing," Hilda said, glaring at Uncle Charlie, who ignored her. "He hasn't got away with a single blessed thing in his life."

I ran to Aunt Erica's car where I had been playing with my turtle after Catherine and I got back from our walk. Holding the box carefully in front of me, I ran back to the truck. Hilda was climbing in the front seat.

"Can I ride in the back of the truck going up the hill?" I asked Aunt Erica. "It'll be going real slow."

"Well, go ahead," Aunt Erica said. "But you hold on and stay sitting down. And I don't want to hear you crying to ride home back there."

"I won't. I mean I'll stay down and everything."

"Why don't you ask your Ma if you want permission to do something?" Ma said to me. "You ask me."

"Well, then, can I?"

"Yes, go on, for pete's sake."

Uncle Charlie put his pickup in low gear and started grinding slowly up the dirt road. The truck shuddered over each bump, its wheels spinning often, raising a thick cloud of dust that hovered in the air like smoke and made the early afternoon sun seem hazy and hotter. The truck nearly slid off the slanting road's crumbling edge several times into the deep ditch on the right, but Uncle Charlie always gassed just in time to spin free. About a third of the way up the hill, in the outer swing of a turn from where the Homestead House's high rock chimney could be seen above the treetops, the truck's underside became hung up across the ridge of two deep ruts. Vince had to hobble on up the road ahead of the others to help rock the truck free. Finally, Uncle Charlie pulled up at the edge of the house's dirt front yard and stopped to let Hilda out. The relatives came out onto the porch and several walked down into the yard waving and calling to us.

"Charlie, you old good-for-nothing, come on in here," Great-Uncle Albert called. He was Aunt Erica's and Grandpaw's only living brother, and was a Methodist minister and a state senator. He walked down the flagstone walk toward the gate; his left arm's stub, which was off at the elbow from a hunting accident, bounced against his side.

Uncle Charlie honked the truck's horn and waved, then pulled back into gear and went up around the road above the house to the low, wrought-iron fence and gate of the family graveyard. I jumped down out of the back to open the swinging gate. Uncle Charlie turned the truck around in the road and started backing across the cemetery, carefully avoiding the headstones, to James' relocated grave up near the doctor's mausoleum. The heavy wheels pressed the grave-yard's grass into matted shiny trenches. I walked behind the truck, helping to direct Uncle Charlie across. I then waited around, watching while he unloaded the tools.

"You want me to help, Uncle Charlie?"

"No, son, that's okay. I'll give you a call if I need you, partner. You run on if you want and play with your cousins."

"I don't like to play with them. I like you better than any of them. And I like Kitty and Grandpaw, too."

"Well, partner, I like you, too. We all do."

"Did you know that Hercules hit me at the picnic grounds? He hit my nose. And it bled."

"No, I didn't know that. I'll see that Henry gets a talking to. I'm right sorry about it."

Strike two.

"Well, Uncle Charlie, I'm going to go down to the house but I'll be back up here to help you. Will you watch out for my turtle for me? It's in that little box in the trunk."

"Sure, partner. You run along and have fun now."

I walked down the hill toward the house. The dark chimneys and upper floor rose like a brooding face over a dense pine stand growing at the field's edge. I followed a sandy footpath through the pines, and when it swung near a small clearing lined with rows of beehives, whose moiling drone filled the air like rain, I started to run and ran until I reached the yard.

The relatives were out in front of the house waiting for the climbers to reach the yard. Aunt Garnet and Aunt Julia, Grandpaw's and Aunt Erica's sisters, stood on the porch waving their aprons and calling hello. Uncle Albert waited by the front gate, admonishing the family to quit dragging their tails and get the dickens up the road. Tom, Aunt Garnet's son, sat on the front steps whittling a chunk of soap and talking with Samuel, Uncle Albert's oldest boy. Several children, my various cousins, played around an inner tube swing which hung from a high limb of the oak growing in the front yard. The oak was very old and large and its branches spread perpetual twilight across the front of the house, and often in the evenings, quick darting shadows of bats flicked in the high limbs.

"Well, I declare, if it isn't high time you folks were getting here," Uncle Albert said as he embraced Aunt Erica with his one arm.

"We can't take time to visit yet," Aunt Erica said. "We got more work to do than you can shake a stick at. We'll have us a nice visit come dinnertime. Well, Julia, old dear, how are you, how are you?"

Aunt Erica walked up onto the broad porch to greet her sisters. Several other relatives had come out onto the porch now, and Aunt Erica went around hugging each one.

"Brother Clint," Uncle Albert greeted Grandpaw. "Are you being sociable on this trip?"

"You still a Harry Truman lovin' Democrat?" Grandpaw asked him.

"I'm afraid I am, Brother. I am."

"Still a teetotaling preacher?"

"Yes, I am that, too."

"Well, I still got no use for you then."

Ma started introducing Vince around to all the relatives, everyone saying howdy-do, and shaking hands, and Uncle Albert said:

"Why, Mary Jane, what did you have to bring the law down on us for?"

"Senator Whitfield," Vince said, "I promise you I won't run you in to the clink till after dinner, if you agree not to spear all the chicken 'fore I get any. And leave me a few potatoes. That way we'll get along just fine."

"And not get to talking politics," Ma said.

"Sheriff," Uncle Albert said, "I give you my solemn word to leave you at least two helpings of potatoes. But I can't guarantee anything about that good old chicken. Otherwise, I'll walk the straight and narrow. And I thank you for the consideration and opportunity. I'll commend you to Attorney General Stevens for the fine judgment and restraint you've shown."

"That old son-of-a-gun Stevens," Vince said, laughing. "Senator, you tell old Doug the next time you see him that you was talking with me and that I let you in on a few things concerning the time him and me went hunting down to Braxton County."

"I'll be sure to mention it, Sheriff," Uncle Albert said.

"I told you windbags, no talking politics," Ma said.

"Well, I guess we'll have to abide, Sheriff," Uncle Albert said.

"A feller knows when he's been told, sure enough," Vince said.

Cynthia and Hercules ran off with the other cousins toward the rock outcroppings, which pushed up through the earth where the front slope hollowed gently before folding into the trees.

"Why don't you run play with your cousins, Speer?" Ma asked me.

"I don't want to."

"You can come stay with me, sweetheart," Catherine said.

"That's just what I'm going to do."

Hilda walked slowly up the wide stone steps onto the front porch and squeezed into a heavy rocker. She picked up an old church bulletin from the green wicker table beside the rocker and began fanning herself.

"My rump is settled for the day," Hilda said. "Or at least till dinnertime."

"Well, you just make yourself all comfy now," Aunt Erica told her.

Tom's and Samuel's wives, Becky and Frances, had come out from the kitchen onto the porch.

"Now, youall have a bite before you set to working," Becky said.

"Well, we had a bite at the Coal River grounds already," Aunt Erica said. "We just have to get to work or we'll run out of light. So whoever is of a mind to work, come on now."

Ma sat down on the front steps and took her shoes off; then barefoot and laughing like a girl, she ran far ahead of Vince down the hard clay path toward the spring. To soak their feet, she had declared, saying they'd be back presently to help work in the cemetery, just wanted to stretch out and rest up a bit after that long ride.

"I expected as much," Aunt Erica said. "A thirty-two-year-old mother acting like a girl."

"Well, dear, she's gay of heart," Aunt Julia said, crinkling her face's wrinkles like paper into a fragile smile. "She was always gay of heart."

"Well, you can be gay of heart and you can be foolish at the same time," Aunt Erica said. "I myself think that you have to be practical to get through life. If you are not practical you can't make do with a blessed thing. And I always say there is a blessing of God about a practical life of making do."

Decoration Day, 1950, contd.

Catherine stopped chopping the weeds around Great-Aunt Susan's grave and stood leaning on her long-handled hoe. She watched Uncle Charlie preparing to mix the cement and sand for the footer in an old bucket. The hair on her arms was damp and dark-looking.

"Well, well," Catherine said. "So this is supposed to be your last contribution to your rock garden, Auntie?"

"Don't go to talking foolish now," Aunt Erica said. She was scraping vigorously at the tangling ivy that grew up the pale marble of the Doctor's mausoleum, making crusty sounds as the vines pulled free. "If you'd set to working as much as talking we'd be finished in no time at all."

"What we need is more help," Catherine said, wiping the perspiration from her pocked forehead with the back of her hand. "What with dear Hilda rocking her rump on the porch and Mary Jane courting down by the spring."

"Where's Ma doing what?" I asked. I was sitting alone higher on the slope in the sun-warmed grass, playing with my turtle. I had been for some time staring at the mausoleum, almost in a reverie, wondering where inside of there the Doctor was and how he would look now, after all this time. It was so mysterious to think that the Doctor, a man I had heard about all my life but had never known, was just a few feet away from me behind mere inches of marble. And there was Aunt Erica, who had known and loved the Doctor for years and years, standing right beside where he was lying. Only she was alive. And he was dead. Would she recognize his face now? I wondered.

"What was that you said about Ma, Kitty?" I asked again.

"She didn't say nothing at all," Aunt Erica said. "You pay no mind to your silly cousin."

Uncle Charlie began to pour the wet gray mixture around the frame footing, then to level it out and to smooth it with his trowel. Sweat glistened in streams down the roping muscle ridges of his stooped back, and beads of water waxed in his mustache and dripped off his nose. His veins, taut from reaching, scored threadlike over his wrists.

"You get that real smooth and even now, Charlie," Aunt Erica said.

"I know what I'm doing."

Aunt Erica stopped pulling at the vines and stood erect. She rolled her fists in the small of her back and stretched, then stood looking quietly out over the headstones that were scattered about the fenced-in section of the field.

"Well, things sure have changed here over the years," Aunt Erica said. "And I'm finished with my share of these things at last. After forty-odd years."

"Why, my dear Auntie," Catherine said, "do you truly believe you have arrested death in this family by planting a rock garden?"

"All you do is talk foolish," Aunt Erica said. "I'm glad Albert didn't bring the fellow from the capital for you to meet after all. You'd just embarrass us all, as usual. You've been nipping ever since we left home. You're killing yourself with that stuff inch by inch."

"Gee whiz!" Catherine said, winking at me. "Do you really think so?"

"Forty-odd years," Aunt Erica said, mostly to herself. "And now, at last, I am done with them. Heavens, but these things have surely cost me a pretty penny, they have."

"If that is the way you feel why did you sink such a bundle here?"

"Heaven only knows, for I don't," Aunt Erica said. "Oh, I truly wanted to get the stones for Mother and Dad and my close kin and all. But getting stones for all these distant kin is something again. But the Doctor, God rest his soul, had his sights so set on it. On getting stones for all the folks. God rest his poor soul. He always worked so hard. All his life. There wasn't a place he wouldn't go to, no matter how remote, if there was illness. And in all kinds of weather. I remember once when he was still riding that old yellow clay-bank mare, he went over Montgomery Ridge to Jeffrey in near-20-below weather. When he got home that night I had to pour boiling water over his boots and stirrups to unfreeze them, so as he could climb off his horse. And his poor old horse was about dead too."

"He was indeed a fine person," Catherine said, quietly. "And a fine doctor."

"Yes, he was both," Aunt Erica said. "He gave birth to I don't know how many babies. I just couldn't begin to count. Enough to fill a town the size of Century twice over. Easily that many. And he worked to the edge of the grave with many poor souls, too. That was the misery of his life. It would just kill him ever single time he lost a patient. For a doctor, he just never accustomed himself to dying as he should have. Back in 1918, when that awful influenza epidemic hit the country, there were so many dead that they had the corpses stacked down in the cellars of the funeral houses. They just didn't have enough coffins. I thought the Doctor would die for sure then from either exhaustion or heartache.

He was a giver and a saver of life and just never accustomed himself."

"When did he die?" I asked. "Was I born yet?"

"He was gone before you came along," Aunt Erica said. "You know, you ought to be a doctor when you grow up, honey. That would be a fine thing to be. A doctor."

"I don't want to be a doctor. I want to have a boat on the river. Like Grandpaw. And be a captain. When did the Doctor die?"

"On December 7, 1941," Aunt Erica said.

"How did he die? What of?"

"You ask enough questions to be a virtual nuisance," Catherine said.

"I do not either!"

"Well, Dick Tracy, your turtle is making a getaway."

My turtle was pushing quickly into the warm grass. I scooted down to it and rapped lightly on its shell. It stopped and folded into itself. The sky, which had been clear since the early morning, began to darken suddenly with clouds. Uncle Charlie looked up and said that there would be rain coming for the evening.

"We'll have to get us an early start for home then, I reckon," Aunt Erica said.

"Well," Uncle Charlie said, "I'm ready to set the stone now. I'm going down to get Tom and Sam to help me get it into place. I just hope we can do it properly considering this unlevel slant we're on."

"Don't start up that stuff again," Aunt Erica said.

"Well, Aunt Erica, if we were down on the level strand where James was buried in the first place, there wouldn't be any problems at all. If you hadn't been so determined to move him up this slope we could get the stone in right-down easy. But that would have been too easy though, wouldn't it?"

"I don't want to hear nothing more about it," Aunt Erica said.

Uncle Charlie headed down the hill, flexing his arms as he walked to loosen up. He stopped once to set up a small, bright cluster of flowers which had fallen over on one of the graves. Then he walked slowly on. His back looked starkly white, silhouetted against the dark pines at the edge of the field.

Aunt Erica had insisted upon having James' remains moved to a spot between the Doctor's mausoleum and the burial plot she had selected for herself nearby. She had had Mr. Ketchum provide for the removal in the first week of May.

"I don't have to justify my doings," Aunt Erica told the family.

"For God's sake, he's been dead and buried near seventy years," Uncle Charlie had said.

"Don't use the Lord's name in vain," Aunt Erica told him.

"Well, they certainly won't find much to move," Catherine said.

"Will he be a fossil, Kitty?" I asked.

"I would not be very much surprised," Catherine said.

"Well, I've heard all I want to," Aunt Erica said. "I am having my little brother's remains moved to where I want them. I just want him lying between the Doctor and me throughout eternity. I can't rightly explain why and what's more I don't have to."

"That corpse you planted last year in your garden," Catherine said, "has it begun to sprout?"

"You quit that terrible talk right this very instant!"

"Will it bloom bloom brightly brightly this year?"

"I said quit that terrible talk!"

Eleven

Graves and burial.

When the Galelareese bury a corpse, they bury with it the stem of a banana tree for company. This way the dead person may not seek a companion among the living.

The Itonamas of South America seal up the eyes, nose, and mouth of a corpse in order that his soul may not escape and carry others away with him.

Before leaving a corpse the Wakelbura of Australia would place hot coals in its ears to keep the ghost within the body, until they had such a good head start away from the gravesite that it could not overtake them.

Grandpaw had once, years ago, worked on a state road construction gang that had paved the old macadam road over East Mountain. They started the grading at the edge of Century, where the old negro cemetery had once been, and when the crew dug into a couple dozen of the sunken, unmarked graves in order to move whatever contents there might be, they found only loose bones, as white and bright as fresh snow from the strongly acid earth. They had spread out a large canvas and had tossed whatever bones they happened to dig across into a single heap upon it. Then, they had carried the canvas on up the hill past the construction area, holding its corners cupped up to keep the bones from spilling. They had then simply tumbled the bones and skulls and fragments into a common pile at the bottom of a common grave which had been hastily dug for the occasion. For a joke, one of the crew members had fashioned a makeshift marker, painting upon it the name of RUFUS TOOFUS POTLUCK. He stuck this over the grave.

Indians of Santiago Tepehuacan believe that if a man ever in his life buries a corpse, he is tainted with the infection of death. From that time on, he is not permitted to plant a fruit tree nor to go fishing with the other tribal members, lest his touch prove fatal to fruit or a warning to the fish.

After raking away the dried stems, Cynthia and I used the brick-circled flower bed in Aunt Erica's side yard for our burial grounds. We had buried two frogs, two mice taken dead from traps we had set ourselves in the attic, cat bones we had found back in the dark under the side porch, and, most recently, the head of a fish which we had found in a neighbor's garbage can. Each time we had a funeral we pretended that it was of a different denomination, such as Baptist or Methodist or Presbyterian or Catholic. Using what details she either knew about firsthand or had pumped from others, Cynthia would devise a basic funeral for each denomination, and then, as the service proceeded, she would elaborate until each one was absolutely unique with its own involved, complex ritual. Around each of our graves we then neatly placed bottle caps and marbles and small stones. At their ends we put little Popsicle crosses that we would have to stand back up after each time it rained.

How you died, Cynthia claimed, determined what your spirit would be like and what it would therefore be allowed to do after death. And since funerals are the main part of dying, at least as far as they determine how you are buried, as a Catholic or Methodist or whatever, all you have to do is get the low-down on them in order to select which kind you want and to therefore control your own ghost, to control where it went and how it got to act when it got there.

Early July 1949.
Jim Lincoln, a thirteen-year-old negro boy who was the grandson of Aunt Erica's maid, Isabel, was mowing Aunt Erica's grass. Cynthia and I were supposed to be helping him by raking the mown grass into piles. We spent most of

the time, however, in playing chase games with him. We would run back and forth in front of his lawnmower, jumping quickly from its path in the very last instant. Sometimes, Jim would pretend to chase after us while we scrambled for the safe base of the piles of raked grass.

No one was certain about how it actually happened. Apparently, Jim, who was barefoot, slipped backward on the slick grass while running and pushing the mower before him. When he started to scream I ran like hell into the house and did not come out again until after they had rushed him to the hospital. According to Cynthia, who had remained to watch the whole thing, it had taken Uncle Charlie nearly ten minutes to disentangle Jim's foot from the mower's blades, all of which time he was screaming terribly and was being held down out of the way by Aunt Erica and Isabel.

I could not believe Cynthia at first, not even when she unfolded the small piece of newspaper in which she had carefully wrapped it to show me. Not until I looked very closely, distinguishing the nail, did I actually believe that it was Jim's toe.

We buried it in the very center of the flower bed, giving to it what in Cynthia's mind was a negro funeral, during which we moaned and clapped and sang a great deal.

When a funeral is passing their home the Karens of Burma tie their children with a special sort of string to a particular part of the house, lest the souls of the children should leave their bodies and go into the corpse which is passing.

A Karen wizard is reputed to have the power to catch the wandering soul of a sleeper and to transfer it into the body of a dead person, the latter therefore coming to life again as the former dies.

In 1883, Colonel P. W. Norris, sponsored by Cyrus Thomas and the Smithsonian Institute, entered the Kanawha Valley of West Virginia in order to excavate and study the ancient Indian burial and effigy mounds and the earthen works which were to be found there: vestiges of the magico-religious instincts of the Mound Builders, a prehistoric woodland culture whose tribes once settled throughout the Mississippi drainage basin and southeastern states. At the time of Colonel Norris' expedition, there were many such remnants to be found, still serving their dead, repeating the memory and mystery of their dead from century to century. Repeating, that is, until the present century, for now things have changed. And most of those sites studied by Colonel Norris are now either severely altered or are gone altogether: the constructions of an ancient people buried deep beneath concrete and steel, and their relics and bones carried away, stored in glass cases in the corners of our better museums.

For example, the Great Smith Mound, which was originally located in the present-day city of Dunbar, West Virginia. When Colonel Norris sunk an exploratory shaft from the mound's top, he discovered a number of skeletons at different levels from different eras. Five were found in a log vault at nineteen feet. The centrally positioned burial of this vault was extremely rich with grave goods, having six copper bracelets on each wrist, a reel-shaped copper gorget, three lance heads by each hand, 100 small seashells, 32 shell beads, and three sheets of mica by its left shoulder. A burial, obviously, of a great chief. According to Norris' measurements, this mound was 175 feet in diameter and 35 feet high, making it one of the largest of its kind. In the 1920s, the top was leveled for a bandstand and then, in the mid-1940s, the whole mound was bulldozed away by the city in order to build a tennis court for the local high school.

We were going to decorate the fraternity house for a Halloween party using a "haunted forest" motif, for which we

would need a lot of greenery. The extensive grounds of a
state mental hospital which was on the outskirts of town
had many evergreens. Some of the finest, oldest trees bordered on a road which ran along the south end of the
grounds. We went twenty-strong one night, and within an
hour we had stripped two dozen or so of the trees. We decided we would also need flowers, preferably the sort found
in those metal or wicker baskets which are used to decorate
graves. On the next night we entered a local cemetery. We
had to climb over a low brick wall. We were drunk as lords.
I don't recall how it actually started but soon we were running and shouting among the graves. We overturned any
headstones in our path that were not too heavy. Also, we
carried away several of the smaller monuments, many of
which had little stone lambs perched on their tops or carved
on their surfaces. The party was a great success. We voted
to use the same motif the following year. We stored the
stones in the attic in order to use them again.

Graves, contd.

When I left Cleveland to return to West Virginia in order
to reenter college, Finus decided to cruise along with me. To
save money we hitchhiked, leaving early on a Monday morning to catch the truck traffic. We had lousy luck, however;
and we had covered less than two hundred miles when late
that same night we found ourselves walking in a heavy rain
along some lonesome country road. We had walked for several miles without a single car passing us when Finus spotted
a small frame church back in a pine grove off the road to our
right.

After trying for a time to pick the lock, Finus had at last
said fuck it, and had simply given the door's old latch several
swift kicks with his heavy combat boots. Once inside, I took
a small flashlight out of my bag and Finus and I headed into

the church's pitch-blackness to look around. Finus started making wisecracks as he stumbled around the dark room about the place being haunted by the Holy Ghost and about us waking the Lord up and having Him take shots at us like we were low-down burglars or something. On top of a piano near the front of the room I found a box of candles. I took a couple of the candles and, after locating a likely spot back in a corner away from any windows that could be seen from the road, I lit them. Then, after making little, melted puddles of wax on one of the backless benches which served for pews, I nudged the candles' bottoms securely into them.

Finus came on over then and both of us stripped off our wet jackets and shirts and spread them out over a bench. We took dry shirts out of our bags and put them on and we both also put on sweaters. We unrolled our sleeping blankets and put them end to end along the wall. Then, dragging-ass tired and still cold, we just sat there quietly resting and watching the thin flames of the candles flicker in the draft. Finus fired up a joint and I could see the pale form of its smoke curling quickly upward. He passed it to me. Above us we could hear the dull thudding of the rain on the tar shingles; and, often, from up among the unfinished beams of the rafters, came the faint flick of wings, bat wings I guessed. I had a sudden picture of a rabid bat swooping down from the darkness and getting tangled in my hair and I gave a slight shudder. Finus clicked on the small, red transistor which he carried with him everywhere. After dialing in strange patterns of static for a time, he finally picked up a local hillbilly station that was playing a Hank Williams tune called "I've Seen the Light," and we both started laughing until tears came to our eyes. We had some dandy dope all right. Finus got a pint from his bag and we started passing it back and forth. Soon it was gone. We started another, again passing it between us. Finus drank with long pulls, holding his head back to swallow deeply, the small glowing bubbles gathering quickly about the bottle's neck. I drank more slowly.

For a long time we sat like this, smoking dope and drinking quietly. Then, after a while, Finus began talking, but as much to himself as to me. This was something he did often when drinking heavily and too quickly. I didn't say anything in return. Nothing was expected. As usual at times like this, he was rapping about the three people he had killed in Vietnam. Two he had shot at close range, a woman and an old man. The other, a young man, he had killed with a knife. He had cut off the ears of all three for trophies. He talked mostly about the man he got with the knife, speaking at length about how the blade had felt different in his hand each time it had entered the man's body in a new place. I could never figure out exactly how Finus felt about what he had done, for his voice was emotionless. He described these events clinically, as you might describe an interesting experiment.

I was really wiped out from the long walk in the rain, and soon the even drone of Finus' voice and the sound of the rain on the roof had put me nearly to sleep. At first I was only half aware of his movement. Then, when I heard the shattering of glass, I was quickly awake. Although the candles were still burning I could see Finus only dimly as he moved about the front of the small church, methodically kicking at anything that drew his attention. I had seen him like this often enough and so I only watched his progress in silence. After a time he stopped and just stood there breathing heavily. Then, after resting, he started to stumble along the communion bench, pissing over its glass racks. I rolled over and went to sleep.

At the first sign of light I woke up. After looking around I found Finus in a small graveyard near the church. It was an old graveyard, somewhat overgrown, with many sunken graves, and with a number of its headstones' inscriptions worn away. The cemetery had only one mausoleum, a small, one-coffin, sandstone-looking affair, also ancient in appearance. Finus was sitting there upon it, swinging his dangling legs. He grinned when he saw me coming toward him. He asked me if I wanted to take a look at a dude who had been dead for over sixty years. As I came nearer to the mausoleum I saw where Finus had chipped and pulled away a large section from one end.

Graves, contd.

The easiest route to the rock cliffs where Mary and I planned to picnic was up through the cemetery at the edge of town. Because the day was warm and because we were in no big hurry, we took our time walking up the slope among the gravestones. We began to make a game of looking for the oldest dates. Here and there we stopped to read one and to wonder about the person whose name was carved on the stone. Each time we stopped I took a big juicy swig from our bottle of wine: good old cheap red wine, unchilled and sticky sweet. Also, of course, we always kept a joint glowing. Mary looked very beautiful. Her bare arms were brown and strands of her bangs were pasted against her damp forehead. Every time she brushed near me, I could smell her, a delicate perfume and faint sweet sweat scent.

As we continued slowly up the hill I told Mary about the way I had once heard Catherine describe a graveyard as some sort of strange living rock garden. It was as though the stones were planted there, Catherine had told me. As though in the dead of night some sort of creatures come out to plant magical pebble seeds: seeds which sprout into stone flowers and blossoms.

Mary saw the funeral tent before I did. She told me that she had never been to a funeral before, that she had always refused to go to one. She was curious and, since no one appeared to be around, we walked over to the gravesite beneath the tent. Apparently the burial service was to be held quite soon. Artificial grass was already spread out about the grave's opening and several rows of metal folding chairs had been placed parallel to one side.

So here we are at last. This is that grave I mentioned so many pages ago. That grave I fell head over heels into and from whose bottom I looked up to find Mary's beautiful face peering apprehensively down in the darkness toward me.

Listen, since it has a lot to do with what happened at the gravesite that day, I would like to describe Mary briefly once more. In the mornings I would usually wake up before her and I would just lie there then and watch her as she slept. Through the open window the morning air would press gently into the curtains, and as they moved, light would flow across her face and over her throat and breasts. Her breasts. Mary's breasts. When she lay on her back with her arms up over her head, relaxed in sleep, her breasts spread softly over her chest, seeming smaller than they actually were, girlish almost. I would watch them rise and fall with her breathing, and I would think about the hands and mouths of all those clowns who had touched and kissed them. Dear old Mary's breasts, her tits, her boobs, those beasts tore me up. It was only because of her beauty, though, that I felt like I did. Or rather, it was because of her beauty that she could make me feel the way she could. Dear old Mary Mary.

After we had stood there for only a few moments looking down into the open grave, Mary asked to leave. But I told her to hold up. There was no big rush. And we were not quite finished with this old hole yet, I told her. Then I made her sit in one of the folding chairs on the front row beside the grave.

Get ready, I said, because we're going to get a million laughs out of this old hole yet.

I told Mary to imagine that she was sitting in a ringside seat beneath the big-top tent of a fabulous circus and that she was just about to witness a death-defying performance that had thrilled the courts and cunts of kings. With several long pulls, I finished off the remaining wine. Then, with a grand flourish of gestures, I started flipping the empty bottle into the air and catching it as though I was executing a juggling act of much difficulty. And then, for my symbolic punch line, I started jumping back and forth over the grave's opening.

We have here one dead soldier of a bottle, I told Mary, while I stuck out my tongue and rolled my eyes and tried to twist my face into weird, rubbery clown grimaces.

I asked Mary if she thought that Catherine's little night creatures would object if I planted just this one small empty dead soldier in their rock garden. Mary did not reply. There was nothing for her to say. She had an idea about what I was getting at, I'm sure. I just kept on hopping around and flipping the bottle and blubbering terrible puns about grade-A holes in which things were planted by magic ho ho. I made half-ass jokes about Leda and about the Virgin Mary, ho ho. My luminous head was reeling with all the cheap, easy signs and symbols I had ever had the occasion to stumble across. I was pulling asshole archetypes out of left field. I was in top form.

Mary Mary   quite contrary   how does your garden grow?

And Mary Mary just sat there, so beautiful. She just sat there watching me with her pretty hands folded in her lap like a young girl at her first prom waiting to be asked for her first dance. O shit! And she was so goddamn beautiful, you see. Of course you do. And she was knocked up, as the saying goes, with some other clown's goodies, his cookies, his jazz, his sperm count. O what the shit, I went on honking around, making beautifully bad puns about cunts and holes and graves and wombs and tombs, and although Mary Mary did not understand much of my symbolic esoteric bullshit, she knew well enough what my act was up to.

Ah, Sid Caesar. Ah, *Show of Shows*. I backed off from the grave and with a neat move made a high deft hook shot with the empty bottle. Its bright green glass shivered with sunlight as it arced, then fell, suddenly, into the heart of the dark hole.

Plant   Plant   Plant, I told Mary Mary.

Still, she did not say anything. She just sat there at ringside, her blue eyes on me, my motions.

I knelt at the edge of the grave and started calling down to the pretty green dead soldier. I asked it how it liked its very special hole. I asked if it had had a happy happy funeral. Oops.

Head over heels, as the saying goes.

I fell. Down, down.

Ah.

Boo.

Twelve

Decoration Day, 1950, contd.

After dinner I headed out to the back porch to get my turtle. When we had finally come down from the graveyard, Catherine had put the turtle and its box up on top of the old icebox at the end of the porch so that the cats could not get to it. Cats were always trying to sneak around and get at things, she had said. That was why at home she would never allow any around, in case they would get to her birds. We had ripped up handfuls of field grass to put in the box and Catherine had said she was certain that the turtle was very comfortable and quite at home. I had whispered the secret name to her, and she had whispered back that "Snake-hunter" was a dandy name for such a handsome old turtle.

I stood on tiptoe to reach the box, then I sat down on the top step, placing it beside me. I watched as Aunt Erica and Catherine and several of the aunts headed down the clay path carrying pails toward the spring where the blackberry bushes were. The cousins were calling and laughing from the front yard. At least a dozen chickens were scattered around pecking in the dirt. They were the ugliest birds in the world, I thought. Catherine had once told me how they would gang up together, attacking any ill or diseased one among them to cull it out. They were smelly all right.

Against the far wall to my left a large wooden crate rested on its side. Inside, among the folds of an old blue blanket, was a cat and a batch of kittens. I went over to the crate to take a look. The large white she-cat was curled into a crescent moon curve and her kittens, five I counted, pressed and pushed toward her pink belly's row of teats. I watched as an especially small kitten, with just a shadowed haze of black fur, tried again and again to reach its ma's milk. Finally I just jerked a large bright yellow kitten away and positioned the small dark one at the sucking place.

—Don't be a fool, a voice said from the kitchen.

—Hell, why not tell the old bitch, another voice said.

—Yes, you just go ahead and see if she don't go straight to Charlie.

—Well, I'm so goddamn tired of her nosing around. All she's done all day is nose around.

—She'll go hollering to Charlie. Mark my words.

—I don't give a damn anymore. Vince said things would be all right.

—Well I'll bet Vince still don't want a scene.

Vince again, I thought. That greasy shithead.

"Just what do you think you're doing?" Hilda said.

She came out through the kitchen's torn screen onto the porch.

"Were you getting your little ears full?" she asked me.

"What are you doing out here, Speer?" Ma asked, as she followed Hilda out the door.

"I'm playing with the kittens."

"I just bet you was," Hilda said. "Mary Jane, this kid of yours needs some good straightening up. Needs his tail jerked."

"Speer, were you out here listening to us talk?" Ma asked.

"You know he was," Hilda said. "He's always snooping around. Just like some nosy old lady."

"Were you, Speer?" Ma asked again.

"I was just playing with the kittens, I already told you."

"Well, you go on out with your sister and cousins and play, you hear?" Ma said.

I picked up my turtle and walked out into the yard. In the late afternoon sun's bright glare the shadows of the trees and rocks sprang thin and long across the ground. I carried my turtle on around the house and down through the front yard toward the rock outcroppings, where the cousins were playing their games of fort and attack. I sat on a wide, moss-patched rock and placed my turtle in its center. I watched the cousins playing, their faces like white moths among the dark trees. I waited.

Willy Bob, Uncle Tom's youngest boy, was the first one to notice me and walk up the hill to where I sat.

"What you got there, Speer?" Willy Bob asked. He stood beside the rock, brown and bareback, looking down at me. His small round stomach poked like a bounced ball over his belt.

Aunt Erica had told Hercules and me to keep our shirts on no matter what the others did because that was just the way to catch your death of cold. But I didn't want to take my shirt off, anyway. And I knew with delight that Hercules didn't want to go bareback either, or rather, that he really wanted to but wouldn't even if he got the chance. Old Hercules and his fat quivery white skin.

"Looks like a turtle you got there," Willy Bob said.

"Yeah, it's a turtle. Grandpaw got it for me. It's got a secret name."

Willy Bob had on blue jeans. And all the other boy cousins had them on also, even Hercules. Everyone but me wore them. Aunt Erica made me wear shorts and leather shoes with strings that were too long and always came loose unless I tied them in knots.

"What's so secret about its name?"

"It's an old timey name that only Grandpaw knows. And now me. Of all the people in the world we're the only ones that know that name. It's like a signal for us."

"Tell it to me, why don't you?"

"I can't because Grandpaw made me swear to keep it a secret. I can't tell anybody. Grandpaw said I might even have bad luck if I told it. I might even die. Or get killed even. It's something to do with magic and stuff like that."

"Well, he told you, didn't he?"

"Yeah, but that's different. He knows how to handle the magic stuff. He knows all kinds of secrets."

The other cousins had walked up the hill now to my rock and they stood about with Willy Bob looking down at the turtle.

"What you got there?" Cousin Dean asked.

"It's a turtle with a secret name," Willy Bob told the other cousins.

"What's its secret name?" Dean asked.

"He can't tell 'cause it's got stuff to do with magic," Willy Bob told everyone. "His Grandpaw told him it."

"I can't tell it," I affirmed. "I would if I could though."

"He hasn't got no secret name," Hercules said. He stood at the edge of the group, picking up rocks and tossing them down the hill.

"Yes it does," I said.

"So what?" Hercules said. "Anybody can make up a dumb name and say it's secret. Big deal. That's dumb."

"Not this name," I said. "Grandpaw told it to me himself and said that it was so old timey that not another living soul knew it. It's as old as the pyramids over in Egypt. And it means all kinds of extra secret things too."

"Like magic and stuff," Willy Bob said.

"Boy, that's really dumb," Hercules said.

"His Grandpaw told him," Willy Bob said.

"Who cares," Hercules said. "It's still dumb, just like he is."

"Are you calling Grandpaw dumb?" Cynthia asked Hercules. She had just walked up the hill behind the others.

"No. I'm calling him dumb, is who I'm calling dumb," Hercules said, pointing to me.

"Don't you go picking on him now," Cynthia told Hercules. "He's just a little kid."

"I'm not doing nothing to the little sissy poo poo," Hercules said. "I'm just minding my own business and chunking rocks is all. I'm chunking them down the hill at the snakes."

"What snakes are those?" Dean asked.

"The ones that come out of the woods when it starts

gettin' dark," Hercules said. He lifted a heavy rock with both hands, then swung it underarm, crashing and bouncing down the slope.

The arriving spring evening had leveled like fog onto the mountain. The damp odor of the woods hung out in the thickening air like fresh wash, and sounds began to click from the high grass and from the trees and from under the dark rocks. And the shadows began to broaden like spreading webs of oil and look black and slick.

"I jus' bet they do," Dean said.

"They do all right," Hercules said. "Every night they do. They come out all over the place. They like to hunt while it's night 'cause they can see in the dark."

"I didn't know that," Willy Bob said. "We might get bit or something."

"Not while I'm around you won't," Hercules said. "I can bust them with rocks. I'm the best rock tosser on Kanawha Street."

"Except for me," Cynthia called from where she sat with Sally, another cousin, under a nearby tree. "I can aim lots better than you or anyone."

"Yeah, but I throw harder," Hercules said. "There's one right there."

Hercules tossed a rock near my foot.

"You just watch out," I told him. "You about hit my foot."

"You best not hit him," Cynthia called and shook her doubled-up fist at Hercules.

"I was only chunking at a snake."

"I didn't see no snake," Willy Bob said.

"There's no snakes out," Cynthia called. "He's just acting goofy to get attention is all."

"No I'm not either! I saw it all right," Hercules said. He swung a heavy egg-shaped rock up to his shoulder, supporting and balancing it there. "I know all about snakes around here," he said.

"You don't know anything," I told him. "And you don't

take your shirt off 'cause your fat skin is white and quivery like jelly."

"As a matter of fact, I see another snake right now," Hercules said.

He pushed the heavy rock from his shoulder. I watched it in the air. Almost like slow motion it seemed to float up, then looping into a small arc, it started down. The turtle's shell sounded like a dropped egg. Just a faint, almost gentle crunch when the rock crushed onto it. Everything seemed to suddenly freeze. Nobody said anything. It was so quiet. I realized that I was waiting expectantly for a cry, a scream, for the turtle to call out in pain, and I was vaguely disturbed at the heavy stillness. No, I was embarrassed by it. Why doesn't someone say something, I thought. I realized that everyone was looking at me, that something was expected of me. But what?

"Hey, you went and busted Speer's turtle," Willy Bob finally said, almost in a whisper.

One of the cousins giggled.

"Well, I didn't mean to," Hercules said. He was grinning.

"That was mean as hell," Cynthia called and ran at Hercules. She grabbed him by the back of his shirt and pulled him down.

Hercules rolled over backward, then sat up.

"Hey you quit that!" he said. "I'm gonna tell for that! I didn't mean to hit his dumb turtle! I was tossing at a snake!"

"There wasn't any snake," Cynthia said. "Except you."

"There was too!"

"I didn't see it!"

"Well, you were sitting over under the tree!"

"I didn't see no snake," Willy Bob said.

"It went under the rock!" Hercules said.

Someone giggled again.

"Stand up and take your medicine!" Cynthia told Hercules.

"That's not fair!" Hercules said. "I can't fight back with you! If I hit you I get whipped for it!"

"Roll that rock off and let's see it," Dean said.

Many giggles.

I started up the hill. I wished that I had long pants on. Blue jeans like all the other cousins. If I had blue jeans on they could not see the way the insides of my stupid knees lumped toward each other. My turtle hadn't made a sound. Nothing at all. My stomach felt strange: cold, like after drinking spring water too quickly; hollow, like that Saturday Aunt Erica had given me a worm pill in the early morning and I wasn't allowed to eat anything until the Alloy Plant's shift whistle sounded at noon, and my stomach had growled with hunger but with not-hunger also. But with the feeling and knowing of the something strange happening inside myself, and my happening insides seeming to twirl over and over. And my face feeling bright.

—Go on and turn the rock over, I heard Dean say again.

—Ugh!

—Ugh!

I felt the cousins' eyes on me. On the bare backs of my legs. Those creeps. I kept my stupid legs as stiff as I could and bent my stupid pigeon-toed feet outward. I walked slowly up the hill. Those creeps. I strained my legs outward until they hurt and several times I almost fell down. If I could get up as far as the old oak they wouldn't be able to see me anymore. My legs or my wet pants. Lightning bugs winked like small hot eyes in the dark air.

—He's gonna go tattling, I heard Hercules say.

—You shut your fat mouth or I'll bust you again, Cynthia said.

—Well, there was *so* a snake!

It didn't even make a single noise, I thought. But maybe turtles didn't make sounds. Maybe they don't even have voices. I could not remember hearing the turtle make any sound at all. Will it be dead? Grandpaw had said that it wouldn't die until nightfall. That you could cut its head away and everything, but that like a snake it wouldn't die until the sun went down. I looked up through the high branches at the sky. The darkness had not completely fallen yet and so the turtle was still alive. It could still feel and hurt. And it could not cry. Old Snakehunter. Good old Snakehunter.

—You get dark, you! I gritted through my teeth at the sky. You get dark right now!

I should have hit Hercules' ugly fat face with a rock, I thought. And he would have fallen on the ground and cried like a sissy baby. And I'd laugh at him and spit on him. And I'd pee on him. Right in his fat face. If I could I would.

But I could not have not even if I had had the chance. I'll stay up by the tree, I thought. And then no one could see. No one could see how I had peed in my dumb pants like a stupid kid.

I had avoided the outhouse all day, with its terrible black hole waiting like a gaping fish mouth, and the rough boards and the nail heads scratching up, cold and hard. I had had to shit almost from the time we first arrived but had held it. Then, later, when I had had to pee I'd held that too, afraid that its relief would set the whole mess in motion. Well, it was too late now. At least part of it was. I was just lucky that everything didn't come at once. Up by the tree in the shadows, though, no one would be able to see, and after a while it would dry. Or maybe I would get a chance to get to Catherine. If it got dark enough soon and if Catherine came out onto the porch, then maybe I could make it to her, safely.

—Get dark up there, you! I gritted at the lousy sky.

I ran the final few yards up the front yard to the tree then fell on my knees among the dark roots. The men were sitting up on the porch in the wicker chairs and rockers. I was afraid

that if I started around the house someone might call for me
to come up on the porch. So it was really best that I stay put.
I sat picking at the black bark of the oak. I remembered how
all the trees at the picnic grounds had had whitewashed
trunks, and the larger ones had whitewashed stones, smooth
and round, circling their bases like rings of resting shell-up
turtles. That had looked stupid. They did not look right,
somehow, painted white like that. They had not seemed real
or something.

A large red ant carrying a leaf bit crawled up on my hand
and I bent close trying to watch it. When the ant reached my
wrist I quickly pressed on it with my thumb. The ant's small
front limbs scratched up as though reaching toward my close
face from the smear of its hind sections. I started to press it
again and I raised my thumb, aiming it. To press the ant
until it was completely dead. But I did not. I just watched it
until finally it got still on its own, with two of its forelimbs
clasped like it was praying. Maybe old Snakehunter was
dead, too, now. I looked up into the darkening, darker, sky.
The ant hadn't cried out when it was killed either. If things
like turtles and ants couldn't cry or scream, could they hurt
then? It seemed like if they could be hurt, they would be able
to cry or something. That only seemed fair. But sure they
hurt. They hurt all right. Everything hurts when it gets killed.
And since I killed the ant, I hurt it. And it was just like the
turtle with the rock crushing its shell, and like all those other
things I had at one time or another seen Hercules kill. And,
boy, could I remember a lot of them. Like that black beetle
Hercules had flipped over onto its back and had crushed its
little churning legs and then had slowly cooked away its underside with matches. And like when I watched him sprinkle
salt all over a moist fat worm and it had slowly writhed into
a shrunken jelly. Or like that morning we had come across a
lizard sunning itself along a rut of the Old Clay Road, and
had moved quietly near enough to look at it, the strange
sleeping smile, the pulse at the throat, its scaly tail folded like

a hug to itself. Then Hercules had stoned it to death, its juices shaping thick and dark around the road's little pebbles. There were so many things killed like that. There were so many things dead. You just couldn't keep count.

Another ant moved up onto my hand. I leaned near again. It found the crushed red ant, circled it, touched it, then began to pull it loose from my skin. I watched as the second ant carried its burden down my middle finger. I wondered if he was going to bury his friend. Or maybe the red ant was a relative or some shit, if ants had relatives. And I wondered if maybe the other ants would wonder why the big red ant was dead or how it was killed. And do ants have cemeteries somewhere deep under the ground?

I heard Catherine and Hilda come out onto the porch.

"Move on over in that swing," Hilda said to Uncle Charlie. "Make some room."

"I'll do my best," Uncle Charlie said.

Now was my chance to get to Catherine.

I stood up and thrust my hands deep into my shorts' pockets, noticing that if I pressed my hands outward and toward each other it helped to hide the wet stain. I walked slowly up toward the porch, turning as I walked at a slight angle, as though I were looking off toward the woods across the road. A clean smell of resin came from the pine trees around the edge of the yard. There was a light breeze with the feel of coming rain in it. When I reached the steps I turned and faced the yard and began gazing intently down the hill toward the trees and rock outcroppings. Slowly I started to back up the steps. The grownups were talking. Maybe no one would even notice me.

—That liquor bill won't ever get through, Uncle Albert was telling. —As long as the Christian people of this state stay united against it.

—Seems to me there's a lot of other things could stand

some attention besides liquor bills, Uncle Charlie said. —
Like state house corruption.

I reached the middle step. Most of the aunts had not
come up yet from picking blackberries and they could come
at any time. Or the cousins could come up the hill from the
rocks.

—There's nothing more important for a good Christian
than to fight the rampant evil of liquor, Uncle Albert said.
—To fight broken homes and scattered families. And broken
souls. These are the big concerns of every Christian.

—I'll have to go along with the Senator, Vince said.

—Horseshit, Grandpaw said, and pushed up out of his
chair. —I'm going indoors and get a drink of water before I
puke right off the porch.

—Hell, Dipero, Uncle Charlie said. —There's more boot-
leg in our county than in the whole state.

—Well, now, Charlie, Vince said. —I wouldn't say that.
Why, boy, you don't know the whole facts.

I reached the top step. Just in time. The cousins were
walking up the hill.

Then Catherine stood up and walked toward the door.
"I'd best be getting the things together," she said.

"Turn on the porch light there," Hilda said. "I'll call the
kids. Why, here they are now."

I quickly sat down. I could feel my damp pants sticking
against my legs. Hercules walked up onto the steps. Catherine had gone into the house and clicked on the porch light
which flashed out brightly across the yard. I could see Hercules glaring at me. The other cousins watched me also, their
faces innocently blank.

"Well I guess you went and tattled, didn't you, big
mouth?" Hercules asked me.

I just sat there and kept my mouth shut. That creep.

"I didn't mean to do it, Mommy," Hercules whined.

"Didn't mean to do what?" Hilda asked. "What have you
done?"

"I was tossing a rock at a snake and it landed on that turtle."

"What turtle?"

"Speer's stupid turtle. I didn't mean to and he went and blamed me and then Cynthia pulled me down and hit me."

"You meant to do it all right," Cynthia said. "And you have some more medicine coming yet."

"He's got nothing comin' from you, girlie!" Hilda said.

"We'll see about that, Fats," Cynthia said, and turned to walk down the hill toward the old oak with the inner tube swing.

"What's going on here?" Uncle Charlie asked, getting up from the swing and walking to the top of the steps.

"I didn't mean to," Hercules said.

"You did too," I said.

"All of you be still," Uncle Charlie said. "Now just what happened?"

"I busted Speer's turtle, but I didn't mean to."

"Why you little devil," Uncle Charlie said. "I'm taking a belt to your butt right this damn minute."

"You jus' hold on there, hothead," Hilda said. "Just wait and get to the bottom of this."

"I know our little Henry," Uncle Charlie said. "I know that boy well enough."

"I didn't mean to," Hercules said and started to cry.

Uncle Charlie came down the steps undoing his belt.

"Don't you dare hit that boy!" Hilda yelled. "He said it was an accident!"

I jumped up and made a dash toward the door but Hilda caught my arm.

"Hold on there, you! What's your all-fire hurry, sonny boy? There is more here than meets the eye."

"Let him go," Uncle Charlie said.

"I didn't mean to," Hercules cried. "I didn't do it on purpose."

"Well I'll just swand!" Hilda said. "Just look here what this boy done in his pants. I just can't believe it."

I shook like hell to get free.

"A big boy like him," Hilda said. "Peeing in his drawers like an infant. I'd be just ashamed. Ashamed. Wait till I tell your Ma."

"Why, I thought you was a big boy," Vince said from across the porch.

"Goddamn it!" Uncle Charlie yelled. "That's uncalled for, Hilda."

I could hear the creepy cousins laughing. I fell to my knees on the slick floorboards and Hilda lost her hold on my arm.

"You leave that boy be," Uncle Charlie said.

"Well no boy of mine would be peeing in his pants," Hilda said. "I'll tell you that."

"I never peed in my pants, ever," Hercules said.

The creepy cousins were laughing, laughing.

I made a quick roll across the boards to get from directly under Hilda and then sprang for the screen door, charging through it just ahead of her grabbing hands. I raced through the low dark rooms, my stupid leather soles thumping the hardwood floors. Where is Kitty? I wondered. Except for faint voices from a far bedroom, the old house seemed empty. I ran toward the kitchen. It was empty. Where could Kitty be? Why couldn't she be in the kitchen?

The kitchen was hot and bright. The high-watt bulbs of its ceiling fixture spread a stark, glaring whiteness. Why did I come out here anyway? I ran toward the kitchen table. A mason jar of flowers was in its center. In the hard light their colors looked moist and delicate. What if Hilda came chasing after me? What if she caught me and carried me around to all the grownups to look at what I had done?

I started to race crazily in circles, around and around the

kitchen table. Bright spots began to flare up before my eyes. They bounced off the bare white walls and ceiling. I tilted my head back as far as I could. I kept running. I squinted my eyes. The room felt more and more closed in. The thick flower smells seemed to stuff the air. I started to open and shut my mouth, gulping at breath. I stumbled dizzily toward the pump and tin basin, but it was empty. I started to jerk the pump up and down, up and down, the spots still spinning before my eyes. The pump's water came spurting out heavily into the tin basin. I splashed the metal dipper into the foggy water and scooped the shocking cold liquid to my mouth, letting its chill wetness choke into my twirling insides and spill soaking from my chin onto my shirt front, its touch like frost to my skin. I heard quick steps coming toward the kitchen. I darted for the screen door, letting the dipper rattle to the floor.

The dark kitten—in the instant my first step struck the porch, I spotted at its edge above the steps the small dark kitten. I measured my next two leaping strides perfectly to lead off the kick I swooped up into the kitten's underside, sending it flying out into the night yard. Without breaking stride I kept running toward the heavy darkness of the trees down the slope. I was not tripping at all. My knees weren't hitting each other. I was making a perfect getaway. I was running faster than I ever had before.

run run run run, I chanted to myself, at each jolting step.

I pictured my own white legs flashing like quick white wings through the dark air

run run run

As I skirted the small crest, the outcroppings rose suddenly up into my sight from the black earth like even blacker shapes: like giant shells, I thought, remembering the broken seeping turtle somewhere down in the darkness of that field. I veered sharply off left for the clay path, whose snakelike twisting I followed beneath the heavy overhanging branches toward the outhouse. I'll go there right this minute and pee,

I thought. I'll even sit down on those stinking boards and shit. And it's dark. And I had never seen anyone, not even Uncle Charlie, go down here at night. And without even a flashlight. Blood pounded small explosions behind my eyes and in the hollows of my ears. The outhouse door stood ajar like the thin lip of some strange, black, vertical mouth.

"I'm here to pee   I'm here to pee,"

I yelled, plunging headlong into the blackness and bouncing against the raw boards of the inside wall, falling back onto the floor. I tumbled up, pulling the door and the total inner blackness fast upon myself, then dropped the lockboard into place. The heavy flowing odor seemed moist over my tasting flesh. The hole's hollow blackness waited blacker than even the air. I stepped quickly out of my damp shorts and backed steadily into the hovering blindness. I pushed downward, twisting, feeling the raw splintering and ragged nails.

The sewer rat—that time splashing sounds had come from the bathroom and when we looked we found a rat who had come up through the pipes into the toilet and who was leaping and falling back, splashing, then leaping again and again toward the bright opening air. Aunt Erica had quickly flushed it squirming and turning back forever into the wet blackness.

I pictured a huge rat mouth rising dark and dripping from the lower waste toward me.

Flies flicked through the darkness. I bent almost double into a gripping hug. Flies walked over the bare flesh of my neck. I felt my eyes go away. They seemed to go away and then to look back and they could see me sitting there.

My called name floated down from the path. Called over and over, but softly, gently. Through the cracks in the board walls I could see the flashlight moving within the night air like a small bright moon.

Thirteen

Watching.

Listen, when I was a snot-nosed kid I used to imagine that things were looking at me from the dark in a secret way, as though they wanted to lock their eyes with mine.

I walk from church, the cushioned quietness of the thick maroon carpet seems to enfold my feet, my steps sinking into it like the squeeze feeling of walking over fresh snow. I am cradled in the deep, slow communal movement. I feel drowned in closeness. I shut my eyes. When I open them again, I see directly before me into the settled glass of eyes, of dead fox eyes. It crawls across the broad wool shoulders of Mrs. Decamp, clenching her powdered neck in its peeled red fur. My eyes are in the frozen dark centers of the fox's: my gaze is captive in glass. They look at me as though they know my name.

· A movie: a soldier dead in a trench beside the road. Rain on his face. His open mouth filling with water, running in thin streams from the corners. His eyes open, white, rolled back into his head. Far across the battlefield two women are searching for him. Slowly, they move from body to body, flashing a light on each dead face.

Summer: moths collect on the screen, their small, lanced feet clasping the rusted wire. Their eyes. Swelling from their small powdery faces, black, beady, locked to the light, absorbing it all. Unless I close the window, turn off the light, there is no escape from them. If I close the window my room grows moist with heat and I can't sleep.

A Mrs. Collins, who lived several blocks from Aunt Erica, was found one September day murdered. Her forehead had been crushed in, apparently with a hammer. When they caught her murderer, a drifter who had robbed and then killed her on impulse, he explained that he had covered her eyes with gauze and tape after he struck her because he felt they were watching his every move.

Mary said that since we were in her home city it was her job to show me around. One night she took me to a house in the Cuban section. We were led to a narrow room which, apart from a single row of folding chairs facing a curtained wall, was bare. Soon, others joined us and we were all asked to be seated and to remain very quiet. When the curtain was drawn I saw that we faced a one-way mirror through which we could look into the neighboring room without being seen in return. It was a bedroom. We spent several hours watching the lovemaking of others, including a fat middle-aged white homosexual and a young negro boy.

Once, when Mary and I were walking home from a movie and happened to pass near the end of an alley, we saw three teenage spade dudes working a drunk over. There was enough light so that we had a dandy view of what was going on. The spades good-naturedly took turns holding and hitting him. The appearance of his face was soon altered. The spades let him fall, then started using their feet. They were laughing, obviously flying high on something. They would spread apart his legs and kick into his crotch like they were practicing some weird new dance step.

Mary asked me why I didn't do something. At least I could go for help, she suggested.

I pointed out to her that the man being worked over had red hair. I explained that I had a prejudice against folks with red hair. I could easily stand by watching them get theirs and never raise a finger to help. Besides, I told her, everyone gets his or hers sooner or later. Mary did not seem to get my point.

I explained further to her that I knew there was no meaning, no logic, to my prejudice. And, also, that there was no easy explanation, such as my childhood experience with the red-headed man who had slapped Ma and Cynthia around, which I had at one time told her about. Certainly, this man had not actually stimulated my need for prejudice; he had simply drawn my attention to a possible object. My particular pet prejudice was only an emotional taproot of convenience. And like a primitive's superstition, it was a genuine, a natural gesture of colonization. And since this feeling was not in any way inherited, it was quite comfortably personal. I simply chose to hate red-headed folk when, on occasion, the opportunity conveniently presented itself. And this feeling was always only temporary; it was without any true brooding bitterness at all. Alas, my little pet prejudice most often took the form of a pleasant indifference. It was a feeling I welcomed as one welcomes the safety of recurrence, the sense of ends sealing themselves into circles.

Now, naturally, I did not lay all of this on Mary right then and there. I told her enough though.

My God, just please shut the fucking jive up, Mary suggested.

I tried to make things more clear. I told her that I wasn't about to cruise back in that goddamn alley and get my goddamn ass kicked for some stupid fucking drunk. I was no hot shit hero. Heroes were jerks in my opinion. Besides, I said, directing her attention to the three spades disappearing on down the dark alley, the whole show was over with now, anyway.

Watching, contd.

From my bed I look past the windows into the darkening shadows of the leaves of the maples. Moving with wind, they shift into the shapes of grinning faces that twist dark eyes toward me.

I sit in the large stuffed chair at the foot of Cynthia's bed. Pushing back deep into its softness, I settle myself and quietly watch the room. Father McBeck, whom Ma has sneaked in while Aunt Erica is away, sits beside the bed. He touches at Cynthia's arm and smiles. He is a Catholic priest. Cynthia slowly turns her head to look into his near face. Catholics are low-down bead-squeezers who pray to plaster saints and sin their heads off on Saturday nights, then pay the priests off on Sunday for forgiveness. This is what Aunt Erica says. As I watch Father McBeck and Cynthia, I wonder to myself if she can smell the witch hazel that usually fills the air about his cheeks and chin. As he talks with Cynthia, too low for me to hear, he strokes his fingers slowly over her bare arm as though tracing an invisible line between points on her wrist and shoulder.

At the window, Ma stands quietly; absently, she fingers the sugared edges of the lace petit point curtains. She seems absorbed in whatever Father McBeck is saying to Cynthia. After a time she shuts her eyes and her lips begin to move. Although Ma is only a few feet from me, she seems strangely very far away. I have the weird feeling that I am observing an image of her that has been in some way magnified from far away. As though she is not happening with the room but is apart from it, alone. The more intently I stare, the more rarefied with clarity and sharpness her features become—yet always with that sense of magnified distance. Then, as though I am watching her increasingly from the wrong end of a telescope, her image slowly recedes. Past the window she goes, out into the evening yard under the trees, then beyond. I squint my eyes at her slow going-away. The quiet woman fading out through the window into the evening shadows. Who is she? I wonder. Who is she?

I shake my head. I bounce it furiously back and forth against the chair. In unison, they all look toward where I sit. I sense from Ma's eyes that she is going to start toward me. But, suddenly, before she actually moves, the bedroom door is flung violently open. It swings backward, hitting into the wall. The hall light flares into the dim room. Father McBeck jerks, twisting around from Cynthia, blinking his eyes rapidly in the stinging light. Aunt Erica stands framed in the bright doorway.

I watched the storm clouds bunch and coil into dark beast shapes. Slowly, they ate their way across the helpless sky.

I raked the leaves away from the rain pool's surface. My reflection looked coiled, haunted in the dark water. It was as though I looked at my own dead face. Boo.

Light and darkness.

I have watched insects swarm about a light, flicking blinded and confused from the dark, bright points in intricate elliptical motions, an envelope of moving energy taking a form of its own, its physics a single naked bulb of glowing electricity. The insects don't need that light at all. It becomes a false moon to misguide them and they must enter its gravity and submit to it.

The evening light, Catherine once told me, was so beautiful, so mysterious as to suck your very breath away, when it would flow shadows through a room like moving water. And rainy-day light was like that also, sometimes: when coming through rain beads on a window, it would weave small shadow dots like dark birds across a room and across all the faces that were in that room. That truly was a mysterious-looking thing, Catherine said. The strange masks light could paste as gently as air against faces, masks that touched too softly to be even felt. And flesh would seem like pale wax under them, melting, moving; and you could not feel them and could never know just how your own face looked. How beautiful and mysterious that was, she said. And just plain old everyday light did every bit of it, pulling mysterious things from all it touched, for mysteries just lurked everywhere, waiting only to be enchanted by such magic as spun light. For lights, she told, were like God's very fingertips and helped His magic twine the world together. The whole world! Twined by magic, making things pull together, then push apart, then pull together again, everywhere and forever. Like moonlight waving the sea into tides and pulling nails loose from shingled roofs. The whole world! Magic of the finger-tips of God.

Listen, the darkness is a reality which would change me or I would starve in it. I can't shape it. I can only enter and sub-mit and let myself be accommodated. I can only attempt to choose my place of entry, my angle of slope, my degree of penetration, my precision of movement: movement that will at last come into a shape, a dimension of its own. Darkness is strange turf.

Out past the plank fence and the Old Clay Road at the edge of the woods, Catherine and I made fairy cottages.

—They don't really need a roof, she said.

I went over the bank to the creek for the small blue and small gray stones, as round as I could find and as smooth as round. I pulled the moss up from around the foot of an old oak. Forest velvet, Catherine said, to carpet forest feet. We fixed the stones around in various room shapes and then covered them with moss. Smaller stones we set about to serve as furniture.

—They come out with the moon to dance, Catherine told me. —You have to sneak out when it's dark and hide and watch very quietly to see them.

But I did not intend to go out.

—You aren't afraid of the dark, are you?

—No.

—Well now, just what is it you want? To see them, cor-rect? Well, if you don't go out you will never have the oppor-tunity, will you?

She blew out the candle. Touch the darkness, she told me. Rub the soft fluid of the shadow between your fingers and feel the texture of its darkness. Gently cup a handful and press the coolness against your face and taste it. Open your hand now, she said, and watch the dark waves flow off your fingertips back into the sea of shadow.

Can you hear the hovering trains of the dark queen of God? she asked me. Can you hear her dark gown in angry whirls about the room, parting in flowing whispers into the corners? Can you hear? she asked.

We will search the rooms in the darkness until we find her. We will work each of the old rooms of this house until we find her. We will press our supplicants' sight faithfully before us like glowing oil into the stone-blind darkness.

We will find creatures like memories waiting alive.

We are lost in the deep inner veins of some sleeping beast through whose heavy blood we wade. And there will be no escape for us, ever.

When she put me in the closet, I said,

—I don't see them.

—Oh but you will. They will whisper things to you when they come. You will feel their breath.

—I don't hear them yet.

—You will. You will.

Light and darkness, contd.

Only once did I ever bring Mary with me into the Kanawha Valley to visit Century. She tagged along with Finus and me one fall while we were taking a car trip through southern Appalachia in order to put together a portfolio of photographic studies of the region. We stayed for only a weekend, taking a room in a low-down local motel. I did not contact any of my remaining family in the area. Too many questions were involved. Because of our photographic interests, I spent a lot of time around the river so that I could shoot it in various lights. One afternoon while Finus went to take pictures of a mine tipple, Mary and I hiked to the top of a mountain just east of town in order to get panoramic shots of the valley and river and town. We made something of a picnic of it, taking along a bag of apples, some cheese and bread, a half-gallon jug of red wine, and several joints that I had rolled the night before and, as an experiment, had soaked with Pernod and let dry.

The mountain we climbed that day was somewhat special to me, to my memories of myself as a snot-nosed kid in Century. I had climbed it many times in those days and had spent long hours alone upon its ridges. Mary was not much of a hiker, and we had to stop often to rest as we weaved our way up the steep slope among the trees and the rock outcroppings. When at last we reached the top ridge, I showed Mary the remnants of that ancient wall which had fascinated and perplexed the hell out of me as a kid. It had been constructed by some prehistoric race of Indians as a part of an elaborate earthworks system that had apparently once traced the upper ridges of several mountains for a number of miles. Now, only a few sections remained as recognizable man-made constructions, and even these generally just looked like low, oddly shaped mounds. I had spent a lot of time back then looking through these ruins. Sometimes I had spent hours simply pressing my hands against the earth-matted stones while trying to imagine those hands that ages before had touched the same places. Why, I would wonder, did those ancient people build a wall along the tops of the mountains? What were they building it against? And, more curious than that, which side of the mountain were they trying to protect? Were they afraid, perhaps, that some creatures might awake from the river and stalk into the hills after them?

Although we had not intended to, Mary and I stayed up on the mountain until nightfall. We piled dry leaves at the base of a large rock to sit on, and while the evening darkened, we watched silently down the slope through the limbs of the bare trees as the lights began to come on in the valley below.

From such a great distance as ours, those lights looked so very frail, the bleached halo about each one seeming so small in the smothering resilient darkness.

For a long time Mary and I just sat there quietly, watching the lights blink on and off. Then, without having to talk about it, we took our clothes off. Unhurried, and sightless in the dark, we went through our touching rituals. Mary's skin was cool and smooth, and the clean smell of fall air rose from it. Whenever I moved, the dry leaves scratched my flesh. The rock's surface was rough to my naked back. I felt Mary's small hand cup gently beneath what passed as my scrotum and press upward. I felt the slight tugging of her mouth on my cock. In the high branches of the trees around us, I could hear the dark wind, could hear the ghosts of that haunted hill, could hear them booing all around us like crazy.

Fourteen

R.I.P. Clinton David Whitfield, 1882–1950.

A catamount and a bulldog were to fight in a wired-off pit in the basement of the Ferris Waters Hotel. Grandpaw had captured the catamount himself at the far end of Morris Hollow. Bill Trombly, Grandpaw's friend and sometimes business partner, had supplied the bulldog. The fight was over quickly, with the bulldog grabbing and crushing the catamount's throat. Heavy betting and short tempers led to a fight between Grandpaw and Trombly, which was not all that unusual between them. In this fight, however, Trombly got his with a bottle between the eyes. Grandpaw spent four years in the Moundsville State Prison for manslaughter.

A young black dude insulted a white woman on a downtown street. Because of this, a mob of white men chased him for several hours through the negro section of Century, flushing him out of every hiding place he found. Finally they caught him. He was stripped and tied to a lamp post. There, in the bright circle of light, a member of the mob used a knife on the man's organs. As I said earlier, I have been told that Grandpaw was the one who did this. He was called Mr. Slick in those days. This was not only because he was completely bald but also because of his slick use of a blade.

Whenever, over the years after Grandpaw's death, I was told these and other badass stories about him, I would try to remember how his hands had looked. I would try to remember how they had moved and how they had felt when they touched me. I found that my memory of his hands did not fit the stories I heard of what those hands had done.

On the ride home to Century that Decoration Day night of 1950, I slept in the back seat of Aunt Erica's car. My head was on Grandpaw's lap. I remember, before falling asleep, watching the lights of approaching cars flash over his face. It was raining and I could hear the rhythmic clicking of the windshield wipers and the sound of the tires on the wet pavement. There was always a faintly sour, though not unpleasant, smell about Grandpaw. I remember how that night he would every now and then pat my head gently with his huge hand.

Someone must have carried me up to the front porch when we got home. In any case, I only remember standing there half-asleep, trying to cover my eyes from the bright porch light. Suddenly Grandpaw came down on his knees beside me at the top of the steps. There had been no sound at all except for the thumping of his knees upon the boards. For a moment he was just there like that on his knees, the rest of his body stiffly erect. Then he toppled slowly forward. His head and face bounced on the brick steps nearly to the bottom before anyone could get to him.

R.I.P. Cynthia Elizabeth Whitfield, 1941–1952.

Hold tight around Cynthia's waist when Uncle Charlie pulls fast.

"Pull faster!" Cynthia calls.

The snow slicks around. The white air slides coldly against my teeth. The black trees jerk past the white air. Cynthia's face is wrapped tightly in a red scarf and when she turns her head I can see only her eyes.

"Don't suck in the cold air," she tells me, her voice muffled in wool.

A neighbor is shoveling snow from his walk. He calls out to Uncle Charlie:

"You make a mighty fine-looking reindeer, Charlie!"

Uncle Charlie laughs. He makes a snowball and throws it at the neighbor who laughs also and ducks. Cynthia's hair sticks out all around the top of her snow cap.

Now, of all the things in this little scene I am completely certain only of Cynthia's eyes, deep blue and moist in the stinging air. From above her scarf they look at my face as though from a great distance. And they look perplexed, or surprised, at something. At me, I guess, for being there with her. It is as though she is not dead after all, only far away, and as though our memories at the same instant have happened to return to this moment in some strange conjunction of need.

The wreath on the double-glass front door had two long dark ribbons hanging from it, and in the light morning breeze they rippled like thin black banners. The house was very still. The only sound was of the water dripping heavily from the wet branches of the trees into the dark soaking yard. I was standing alone at the end of the front porch by the swing. They had brought Cynthia back late last night, but greaser Vince would not let me go in to see her yet. Ma wanted to be alone with her, he said. I pressed my face close against the front bedroom window trying to see through the heavy folds of the curtains hung on the inside. But I could not see anything. I could not see either Ma or Cynthia. I could see only the mirrored shadow of my own face and of the trees behind me and even of the houses across the street in the wavy glass.

Mr. Ketchum's hearse was parked directly in front of the house. Rain beads sparkled from its bright chrome. Its shining black metal hazed almost blue in the morning light. When the soft wind shuddered into the trees, leaves, sodden and dark, fell. Several pasted themselves onto the hearse's top and hood.

People began to come. Some of the women brought pies or cakes. Some carried dishes of noodles or baked beans or meatloaf. Mrs. Porter brought a Virginia ham. The Stagmen sisters brought chicken on a large platter covered with greasy waxed paper.

Long pools of dark water formed in the trenches that the cars' tires hollowed in the wet gravel of the cemetery's driveway.

I made too much stupid noise trying to sneak out of the house. Then, when I was trying to climb over the side yard's fence, I fell tumbling onto the other side. For a moment I just sat there in the damp gravel, letting my eyes get more used to the dark. A light suddenly clicked on from the house. I jumped up and ran like hell down the alley. A dumb dog started barking. Others joined in. I stumbled and fell against a garbage can, knocking it over. I got up again quickly and ran on. By the time I reached the Old Clay Road my side was hurting and my legs felt watery. The left knee of my pants was torn and my leg was stinging. When I stopped to touch it I felt something damp and sticky. There were strange sounds coming from the woods all around me. I was too tired out to run again but I managed to trot, and I counted each jogging step out loud, picturing the number as I said it, trying to keep the sounds and the darkness from my mind.

When I reached the tracks I rested, lying out flat in the long grass of the bank. I could feel the dampness soaking through the back of my shirt and pants. The sky had started to clear and as the dark clouds shifted, I could see several pale stars and the moon, which was full and very bright. I heard a train's whistle from far down the tracks so I got up to go on. The rails of the tracks were wet and slick and looked shiny in the moonlight. I crossed each one carefully. To my right, the lights of the town looked like low stars. Except for the train's whistle everything was so quiet. The moonlight made things look soft and luminous: trees, houses, parked cars, everything seemed to glow from inside itself, a strange sheen spreading from some secret inner place. As I walked along the dirt road through the negro shack town, I kept hearing faint laughter, a woman's laughter, brittle as glass. Dogs started barking again and I took out running, and I ran until I reached the flood wall's crest. As I waded through the high grass down the bank to the river, I pretended that I was invisible and that nothing could see me to get me.

I walked along the shore until I reached the secret tree, whose huge, flood-washed roots seemed to twist up like frozen snakes from the dark sand. Against the deep blackness of the cave they formed beneath the tree, the roots looked bleached almost white. I sat down on a nearby fallen log, the same one Uncle Charlie always sat on when we used to come here to fish. I spread the tear in my pants' leg open and touched at the dark smear of blood. The cut was stinging like hell and I tried blowing on it, which didn't help much. I was shivering. I took the butcher knife that I had swiped from the kitchen out of my belt and stuck it in the log where I could grab it quickly. It didn't help much. I took the haunt list out of my pocket and tried to read it over. I couldn't; it was just too dark under the trees. Anyway, I knew the list by heart. I just sat there then and waited. I did not let myself think about the woods behind me or about the darkness. I sat there watching the moonlight as it was broken and gathered by the moving water of the river and I tried to shut everything else from my mind.

"Is that you, Speer?"

I jumped up, looking around. I didn't see anyone at all.

"Speer?"

Then I saw him. He was standing in the weeds higher up on the bank. He walked slowly on down to where I stood.

"You slipped out, son," Uncle Charlie said. "You have everyone back home all upset. Your Ma is crying, she's so worried."

"How did you know I was here?"

"What are you doing running around in the middle of the

night like this? Kind of late for a constitutional, isn't it, partner?"

"How did you know I came down here?"

"Well, I looked in all your other hideouts. Had a hunch you'd be here."

"You didn't tell anyone else about it, did you? You didn't tell that shit Vince?"

"Course not, partner. You know I wouldn't do that. I wouldn't spill the beans 'bout an old partner's best hideout."

He gave my head a couple of easy cuffs. Small moons of light were gathered in the thick centers of his glasses' lenses and I couldn't see his eyes.

"Don't you think it's time to head for home now, son?" he asked, his voice even quieter than usual.

"No."

"I know how you feel, partner. But, son, this isn't going to help any. Coming out here at night like this. Now, why don't we just go on home and fix up a good old hot cup of cocoa? We can sit up and talk."

"No."

"Well, why not, son?"

"Just because," I told him and turned and sat back down on the fallen log.

"Because why, partner?"

"Because I'm waiting."

"For what?"

"I'm just waiting, is all."

"Well, son, about how long do you figure on waiting here?"

"I don't know."

"Well, I can't just leave you out here alone."

"I have to wait."

"I see. Well, then, can I wait along with you?"

"I guess so."

Uncle Charlie didn't say anything else. After a time he sat down beside me. Part of the fallen log we were sitting on was in the river, forming a calm lee of water out of the current. Now and then Uncle Charlie would flick a pebble into this lee, and I would watch as the silent ripples from each pebble spread away and away into the river. We sat and sat and sat.

R.I.P. Catherine Jane Whitfield, 1913–1953.

A winter Sunday afternoon. Catherine and I are sitting in her front room watching the two beautiful white birds, the doves, that she keeps in a gilded cage. They touch feathers and down to one another and coo softly together. After a long time of not speaking, Catherine begins to talk. She tells me that long ago people had believed that souls were like such doves as they fluttered up away at the moment of death and that even St. Benedict said that he saw the soul of his sister issue white like a dove from her dead lips and fly toward heaven.

Catherine was in the sanitarium nearly two years before checking out, and I have been told that she suffered a very painful death. And because she had refused the drugs which would have deadened her awareness of the pain and the dying, she was completely conscious at the end. I wonder if those supposedly grieving people who hovered about her at death could dig why Catherine did this. I wonder if they could realize that, for Catherine, a time as richly privileged as dying, unless strained through consciousness, would have hardly been worth the effort. And how many of them stopped to think that old Catherine had actually ended her trip as she had so often predicted she would; she had—so very literal to her own words—ended it all as pickled as pig's feet in brine. And, as she said, there is nothing like a good stiff sauce to save one's freshness. I have, Catherine said, taken great pains to see to the correct and early embalming of myself, being my very last gesture of colonization. Of recognition.

During the summer following my second year in college, I worked part-time as orderly in the cancer ward of a large hospital, and I have closely watched the eyes of those people who are rolled conscious into a terminal patient room, eyes black with as much embarrassment as fear. I have had the experience of quickly wrapping a dead body in a plastic shroud, binding it tightly, and rolling it swiftly through emptied hallways to the cold storage chambers deep below, in the hospital's basement morgue.

The light in the cancer ward's terminal patient room was always dim. The room was painted a uniform deep green, and what exhausted light there was seemed to spread itself like a thin fluid over the rough plastered walls, walls which always looked faintly moist from this but when touched proved actually cool and very dry.

Once in an early letter of Catherine's to me from the sanitarium, she wrote that it was too expensive, too plush of a place for her to pull off a proper pedagogical suicide: that an abject sacrifice needs an abject joint. I wonder if when they rolled her conscious into the sanitarium's terminal patient room to begin really getting down to business, she still felt the same way about the joint's plushness. I wonder what she thought of walls that seemed to be like some strange green perspiring flesh. I wonder if old Catherine got a kick out of her misjudgment about the joint's plushness. I sure do wish I knew Catherine's final decision about just who the joke was after all on.

Ho ho, Kitty. Ho ho.

R.I.P. Charles Albert Whitfield, 1916–1963.
In the cliffs east of Century there is a strange formation of rocks which was formed by a big shot of explosives on September 6, 1901, while the C & O Railroad line was laying track along the mountain toward Donnally. After the smoke and debris of the big shot had settled, the workmen spotted

this unusual formation high on the cliffs, and they decided right then and there that it looked just like the profile of President McKinley. This was a bad omen, they all agreed. So they were not all that surprised when no more than thirty minutes later the news came in over the telegraph that an anarchist named Leon F. Czolgosz, from nearby Kanawha City, West Virginia, had shot President McKinley while he was attending the Pan-American Exposition at Buffalo, New York.

By the time the high mines at Donnally had finally played out, and the mountain tracks were no longer worth keeping up, the C & O had laid new steel in the bottoms, following parallel to the river up the valley. On one short stretch of this lower track, about a mile east of Century, there is a place from where you can see through the trees up the mountain to the rock cliffs and the McKinley profile. This is the exact spot where they found Uncle Charlie.

Several negro boys on their way to fish that morning first came across him. Or rather, came across his upper torso and his lower torso and legs, because at first they could not find his head. I was told that the attendants who arrived with the ambulance from Ketchum's Funeral Home had trouble collecting the body For one thing, a steep and over-grown embankment was between the tracks and the dirt road up above. For another, Uncle Charlie's body had been roughly severed into three sections, which made handling and securing it difficult. From all appearances, he had been lying cross-ways on the tracks, his neck resting on one rail and his lower body on the other. The attendant who found Uncle Charlie's head where it had been rolled up the tracks, carried it back to the stretcher by the ears. This, I was told, got a few laughs from those on hand.

I did not go to Uncle Charlie's funeral. Instead, on the afternoon it was thrown, I set out along the tracks east of town toward the stretch where they had found him. When

I got there I looked around, but there was really nothing left to see. I had not actually expected to find anything. I determined where the exact spot had been by faint stains on the steel rails and by a tie and some gravel which were still brownish with dried blood.

Although the woods on the embankment above the tracks were dense and were thickly leaved with summer growth, I could easily see up the mountainside to the rock cliffs and the McKinley profile. I wondered if on that night Uncle Charlie had somehow, even through the rain and darkness, known it was up there right above where he was about to get his. Or was it just another one of those crazy coincidences which make life so amusing. I watched the afternoon sunlight through the gathering clouds move shadows across the high cliffs. And the brooding face, with each shift of shadow and light, altered its expression, as though thoughts, feelings, memories were being drawn out of the old stone.

I spent some time looking around along the sides of the tracks, kicking about in the high weeds and in the brush and vines under the trees. In a slight depression under the low limbs of a spruce I found a half-gallon bottle of good old cheap red wine. It was almost a quarter full, was sealed tightly, and was sitting upright in the needle loam as though simply left waiting there momentarily. So what the shit. I picked it up, unscrewed its metal cap, and tried a swig. It was lousy. It was warm and sour and had a couple of cigarette butts floating in it like little dead fish. So what the shit. I took another swig.

R.I.P. R.I.P. R.I.P. R.I.P.

I read once that among the Mbaya Indians of South America the women would destroy all of their children except the one they believed to be the last. Any children born after this chosen one were murdered also. This practice even-

tually depleted a branch of the Mbaya nation, who had been
for many years the most formidable enemies of the
Spaniards.

Among the Lengua Indians of the Gran Chaco the missionaries discovered what they described as a carefully
planned system of racial suicide, by the practice of infanticide, by abortion, and by other methods.

The Jagas, a conquering tribe in Angola, are reported to
have put to death all their children, without exception, in
order that the women might not be encumbered with babies
on the march. They recruited their numbers by adopting
boys and girls of thirteen or fourteen years of age, whose
parents they had killed and eaten.

A newspaper article reported that a warrant had been
issued by the F.B.I. for a twenty-year-old Wac, charging her
with murder in connection with the death of a baby found
wrapped in a blanket and stuffed in her wall locker.

Because they eat garbage and therefore begin to smell
soon after death, carp are usually kept alive for as long as
possible in tanks in the rear of the fishmarket. This was
what I told Mary Mary once, when we happened to stop in
front of a fishmarket's window. We had been walking randomly about the streets near the campus for several hours.
We had been fighting, of course, of course. I had made it
clear to Mary Mary that I was not impressed with her Catholic crap and that as far as I was concerned she had but one
option. We stood in front of the window, silently looking in
at the bins of crushed ice stuffed full with fish. From their
faded scales and from the stained ice, steam rose like cold
smoke to haze the lower glass. After a time Mary Mary told
me that I was something of a cold fish myself. To be more
exact, a cold bastard. I told her that long ago the Egyptian
hieroglyphic symbol for hatred had been the fish.

I told Finus that what I was going to do to him did not
really have anything to do with Mary Mary. In fact, it was
not even really a personal thing at all. Rather, it was simply

a necessary action for me. An event of discovery for me about my own situation. It was, I told Finus, a symbolic and abstract gesture for me. A basic primal motion, that's all.

Although they started dragging for it around midnight, they did not find Mary's body until almost noon of the following day. I told them that I had earned my senior lifesaver's credentials at the Y.M.C.A. before I was fifteen, so I knew what I was talking about when it came to things like water safety. So there was just no excuse at all for me having permitted her to go swimming alone at night in the lake.

Once while taking a long, beer-foamy leak in a bar's head, I read scribbled on one of its walls some graffiti which said that "reality is the shifting face of need." I know from my own experience that the past is the only truly controllable reality. Also, I know from my own experience that there are responsibilities which I owe to myself that begin with my memory.

When they finally got Mary's pale, bloated body to shore, they were astounded at what they found. The two small holes in her throat were weird enough, but when they discovered that her body was drained of all blood, they were beside themselves. It sure was weird all right, I had to agree.

Keeping the ghosts in my ghost story safe, having them always toe the old mark, spooking just where and how they should, haunting me only as signs, as symbols, seldom dangerous or overly terrifying, is a trick I have been trying to master for years, years, relentlessly.

Maybe I don't really know how dear old Mary Mary got hers in the end. Or Finus. Maybe I don't even know if they have actually gotten theirs at all. Maybe they don't really belong in my collection. After all, dead things are my hobby. Confirmed dead things. On the other hand, as I have said, I have responsibilities.

A seance is a seance is a seance. Ghost stories just don't want to end. Ghost stories just keep folding back and back on themselves.

Sometimes I think that my Y.M.C.A. senior lifesaver's credentials are worthless. Sometimes I think that when it comes to things like water safety I really don't know anything at all.

Fifteen

Decoration Day, 1950, concluded.

Catherine led me back through the low, dark downstairs rooms to a small bedroom off the parlor, then had me get up on the bed.

"Okay, Dick Tracy," she said. "How about you hanging out here for a couple of minutes and I will be right directly back."

"I'm sorry about peeing in my stupid pants like a dumb kid. I did it when my turtle got busted."

"Well, don't worry about it. Now you sit tight and I'll be back in a jiffy," she said, and quickly left the room.

I sat quietly on the bed. Its gingham patched quilt was cool against the backs of my legs. I hoped that that shithead Hercules had gotten his ass whipped. Uncle Charlie had been taking his belt off to do just that and I just hoped that he went through with it. I was really tired out and as I settled down deeper into the sinking feather mattress, I felt like I could go to sleep right then and there. The room's only light was from the small old-fashioned kerosene lamp on the circle table beside the bed, and shadows were swollen along the baseboards and in the corners.

Catherine came back into the room carrying a tin basin of warm water with soap and a cloth. She helped me undress and then started to wash me.

"She will never treat you like that again," Catherine said, her voice tight and angry. "I promise you that."

"I love you, Kitty."

"Well, my goodness. I am perfectly charmed. I love you also. What brought that passionate declaration on?"

"Nothing, I guess."

Catherine moved the warm cloth over the rawness between my legs where the wetness had rubbed me.

"Does that feel better?" she asked me.

"Yeah. A whole lot. It was really stinging before. It rubbed me when I ran down the hill."

Uncle Albert came into the doorway and I quickly pulled the quilt over myself. The idiot didn't even knock.

"Don't mean to bother youall," he said. "I just happen to remember this ol' thing."

Uncle Albert held out a turtle. Or rather, a turtle shell.

But it's empty, I thought. There was no turtle in it.

"I found this ol' thing last summer out in the garden and just stuck it back under the house. Forgot all about it till that ruckus out front. Thought maybe ol' Speer might like to have it."

"What is it?" I asked.

"Well, now, it's what they call a shed shell," Uncle Albert said. "An empty shell. Turtles go and shed their shells when they fix to crawl off and die. Something like how snakes cast their skins. Don't come across too many of these here buggers."

"It's not really a turtle," I said.

"No, I reckon it's more just the remains of a turtle."

"It couldn't even crawl."

"No, I don't suspect it could do much crawling," Uncle Albert said and laughed. "But they are a curiosity to find and I thought you'd like to have it. And meanwhile, I'll keep my eyes peeled for a live one for you. This is just a curious piece, is all. Just thought you might like to have it, boy."

"Why yes," Catherine said. "Now you thank your Uncle Albert, Speer."

"Yeah. Thanks, Uncle Albert."

"Why sure. It's nothing at all. I'll keep my eyes peeled, boy," Uncle Albert said as he left the room.

I turned the shell over in my hands to look at it carefully.

"This is the funniest turtle I ever did see," I said.

"Oh, it's a funny one all right," Catherine said. She pulled the quilt back off of me to finish drying. "Well, Dick Tracy,

I'm going to round up something for you to put on. So you just sit here like a good little gangster and I will be right back."

"Well, I'm sure not going walking around without any pants on."

"I suppose not," she said laughing, then left the room carrying the basin and towel.

I sat quietly waiting, like Catherine told me. I didn't mind waiting at all. In fact, waiting was something that I liked to do. It was like you were not happening with things here and now at all, but were happening outside of them. And time seemed to slow down. The quilt felt warm around me and I kept getting sleepier. Calls and laughter from the other kids' play out front stretched through the low rooms to me. They must be having a good time, I thought. The creeps. At least they hadn't gone back down to my smashed turtle and had just left it alone. At least I hoped they had left old Snakehunter alone and hadn't kicked him around or broken the shell up anymore. That was something Hercules was likely to do though. The creep. I could not distinguish any of the calling or laughing voices. Except one. And I hoped that I was dead wrong, because if that was Hercules' high squealing, piggy laugh then it sure didn't sound like he had gotten his stupid ass whipped. It sounded like he had gotten off scot-free. Here he had busted old Snakehunter and everything and he got off scot-free. That wasn't fair at all. Well, I'd figure out a way to get even. I had a few things up my sleeve yet. So let the creeps hoot around and get their laughs. I didn't give a shit. Anyway, I was so sleepy. Everything seemed very fuzzy and the kids' shouts sounded like they came from far away. Like they were coming from miles and miles away. And they seemed somehow like far away in time, too. As though I was hearing them from a long, long time ago. Like a strange memory. Catherine had once told me that memories were like the goblins: were like ghost echoes of time, of the past. And ghost echoes, she told, were like the laugh of Lazarus: like echoes of the raised dead. Jesus brought Lazarus back from the tomb and that was what Catherine meant. When you remembered with all of your heart, you brought things back from the dead. That sounded so mysterious. And somehow it was sad. Like when I would lie in bed and listen to dogs barking somewhere out in the cold night. It was sad also like when I tried to picture myself getting old.

I lay there on the feather bed with the warm quilt around me and tried to picture myself an old man like Grandpaw. Or like one of those old men who sat on the benches at the courthouse and watched as people walked past them all day long. They would sit there bent forward as though with stomachaches, listening very closely to the clicking, moving feet on the bright pavement, listening for a step they might recognize that might just happen to come up to them. A step like a memory to single them out and walk deliberately right up to them. I tried to picture myself bent forward, my eyes watery, my mouth open and loose. Sometimes it seemed like I was already old. Sometimes it seemed like I had been old forever.

Catherine had once said when we passed the seated old men,

—It's a wonder the poor old things don't catch flies in their mouths, the way they are flopped open.

So that was being old. Sitting in the shade on a bench at the courthouse, bent listening, mouth open and loose, waiting, waiting, waiting. I pictured my old self walking, bent and shaking, out through the house to where the kids were playing in the front yard, and they all stopped running and calling when they saw me and just stood there looking at me. Can I play this game? my old self asked. It's a wonder he don't get flies in his mouth, my old self heard Hercules say, and all the kids laughed. I have walked from a long way off, my old self told them. From all the way downtown at the courthouse. It's a real wonder he don't get flies right in his mouth, Hercules said. Flies right in his mouth. Of his mouth. That sounded just like some horrible disease. Flies of the mouth. Old Mrs. Belcher's legs had drawn flies before she died, Isabel had told Cynthia and me, and had explained that old Mrs. Belcher's circulation had gotten so clogged, her poor old legs had turned black just like meat spoiling in the sun and had drawn scatters of flies. But then Catherine had said that no such horrible thing ever happened to poor old Mrs. Belcher at all and that such a tale was only negro fence talk. I couldn't remember Mrs. Belcher much anyway. Maybe I would be old all my life long.

"Wake up, Dick Tracy. Wake up and shine."

"I wasn't asleep."

"Just resting your weary eyes, right?"

"Yeah."

"Well, I just hope to heavens these fit you."

Blue jeans! Hot shit!

"Whose pants are these?"

"An extra pair of Willy Bob's."

"Will I get to keep them?"

"Afraid not, Mr. Tracy. They are Willy Bob's."

"Shit."

Aunt Erica came into the room.

"Is Speer all right now?" she asked.

"Fine as wine," Catherine said.

"Herky busted my pet turtle, is what happened, Aunt Erica. And he hit me too."

"I know all about it," Aunt Erica said. "And I'll see he gets tended to when we get home."

"Will you whip him?"

"We'll see. Here, your Grandpaw told me to give you this. He said it would ease the sting off your nose."

Aunt Erica handed me Grandpaw's black bone-handled pocketknife.

"What does he mean that it will take the sting off your nose?" she asked.

"It's a special signal between just him and me, so I can't tell what it is."

"Well land's gracious. I surely wouldn't want to break in on lodge secrets that are just for menfolk."

"Did he say if I got to keep the knife for good?"

"No, he didn't. But I'm just not sure myself whether you're old enough yet to have a knife."

"Oh, Aunt Erica. Please!"

"Well, we'll talk about it."

"Where is Uncle Clint, anyway?" Catherine asked.

"He's been hopping around too much today," Aunt Erica said. "He's laying down back in that bedroom off the kitchen. That old bird just won't listen to what a body tells him for his own good. Now, what do you plan to do right now?"

"Well," Catherine said, "I thought I would just get this little bugger in some dry drawers and we would go on down the hill to the cars and wait on the rest of you."

"That sounds like the best thing. That little boy has had himself a trying day. I'll be getting the others down the hill right directly. Well, Speer sweetie pie, you be a good boy and try to fall asleep on the back seat, if'n you can."

Aunt Erica left the room. Catherine shook the blue jeans out and unsnapped them. And they had a zipper which she zipped down. A zipper! I had never before worn pants with a real live zipper, although several pairs of my shorts and trousers had a fold of material lapped down the front as though concealing one, and into whose crease I would often press my fingers as though checking.

"Here now, you step down in these. One leg at a time."

"Kitty, do you remember what my Pop looked like?"

"Why, yes indeed."

"Well what did he? Look like I mean."

"You've seen his picture."

"I forget it."

"Well, actually, he looked a great deal like I suspect you

will look one day. Handsome as a movie star. Handsome as Tyrone Power."

"Did he look like Vince at all?"

"Heaven forbid."

"Wouldn't it be nice if you and me could get married some day?"

"I accept! I accept! This is the closest I have ever been. We will begin making plans as soon as we get home."

Catherine led me out the side door from the parlor and down the set-in, stone footpath. When we reached the road she clicked on a flashlight.

"You watch your step now," she said and took my hand.

"You want me to open my knife in case something tries to get us?"

"Well, I don't think that will be necessary. But do keep it handy."

A wind pressed into the trees around us. I held the empty turtle shell up to my ear.

"I can't hear anything in this old thing," I told Catherine. "Like I can the ocean in the big pink shell at home."

"That thing is a poor excuse for a shell all right," Catherine said.

She took the shell from me and turned the light on it.

"This thing is absolutely worthless," she said.

She threw it out into the darkness.

"That pathetic thing would not even be worth taking home for our grand collection."

The lights from the house flared, moving hunking beast shadows out into the front yard and trees. Catherine and I stumbled often as we walked slowly down the rutted dirt road.

"My, my. Just listen to those old spooky woods," Catherine said, and I could sense her shiver.

"To what?"

"Oh, just to all the ghosts and goblins back in there. Back in the dark spooky spooky spooky woods."

So I listened with all of my heart to the goddamn woods. So, boo, goddamn it. Boo.

A Note on the Author

CHUCK KINDER is the author of four novels—*Snakehunter, The Silver Ghost, Honeymooners,* and *Last Mountain Dancer*—and three collections of poetry—*Imagination Motel, All That Yellow,* and *Hot Jewels.*

Kinder was born and raised in West Virginia. He received a BA and MA in English from West Virginia University, where he wrote the first creative writing thesis in school history, which evolved into his first novel, *Snakehunter.* He later caught a Greyhound and headed west to join friends living in San Francisco.

In 1971 Kinder was awarded the Edith Mirrielees Writing Fellowship to Stanford University, followed by the Jones Lectureship in Fiction Writing. He has been a writer-in-residence at the University of California, Davis, and at the University of Alabama, and he is the recipient of a National Endowment for the Arts grant and Yaddo's Dorothy and Granville Hicks Fellowship.

At Stanford, Kinder became close friends with fellow students Raymond Carver, Scott Turow, and Larry McMurtry. His relationship with Carver inspired *Honeymooners.* His struggle to complete that book inspired the character Grady Tripp in Michael Chabon's *Wonder Boys.*

As a professor of creative writing at the University of Pittsburgh for more than three decades, Kinder served as the director of the creative writing program and helped foster the careers of Michael Chabon, Earl H. McDaniel, Chuck Rosenthal, Gretchen Moran Laskas, and Keely Bowers.

He now lives in Key Largo, Florida, with Diane Cecily, his wife of over forty years.